Millersburg Magick Mysteries #1

Spells and Sleuths

Suzan Harden

More Books by Suzan Harden
(Each series is in suggested reading order)

Millersburg Magick Mysteries
Spells and Sleuths
Fae and Felonies
Magick and Murder

Bloodlines
Blood Magick
Zombie Love
Zombie Confidential
Zombie Wedding
Amish, Vamps & Thieves
Blood Sacrifice
Love, War & a Bulldog
Zombie Goddess
Ravaged
Sacrificed
Reality Bites
Ghouls in the Grocery Store
Resurrected
Bloodlines Shorts Anthology
Bloodlines: The First Boxed Set

Seasons of Magick
Spring
Summer
Autumn
Winter
The Seasons of Magick Anthology

Justice
Sword and Sorceress 28
("Justice")
Sword and Sorceress 30
("Diplomacy in the Dark")
Justice: The Beginning
A Question of Balance
A Modicum of Truth
A Matter of Death
A Touch of Mother
A Twist of Love
A Virtue of Child
A Hand of Father
A Measure of Knowledge
A Hint of Thief
A Cup of Conflict

The Justice Thalia Stories
Snowfall
Murder Most Fowl
The Sweetest Poison
A Granddaughter of Mine
Too Many Fish in the Sea

Tales of the Twelve
The Trickster Priestess and the Demon

888-555-HERO
Hero De Facto
Hero Ad Hoc
Hero De Novo
A Very Hero Christmas
Hero De Jure
Hero In Camera
Hero Amicus Curiae
A Very Hero Wedding
Hero Ad Litem
Queer Eye for the Super Guy

Solar System Services, Inc.
Alone Is Not Lonely
Halloween Harvest ("A Place at the Table")

Soccer Moms of the Apocalypse
Pestilence in Pumpkin Spice
Famine In French Vanilla
War in White Chocolate
Death in Double Mocha

Miscellaneous
Sword and Sorceress 31 ("Pig-Headed")
Sword and Sorceress 32 ("Unexpected")
Practical Witches
Revenge Served Hot
The Yule Switch
Chocolate for Dinner
Silver Shoes and Pigs' Ears

For updates, news, and giveaways, join Suzan's mailing list or visit her website at www.suzanharden.com. You can also check her out on Facebook @SuzanHardenWriter.

This is a work of fiction. All characters, organizations and events in this story are products of the author's imagination and are not to be construed as real. Any resemblance to persons, living or dead, is entirely coincidental.

SPELLS AND SLEUTHS
(Millersburg Magick Mysteries #1)
Copyright © 2023 by Suzan Harden

ISBN-13 - 978-1-938745-76-8

Published by Angry Sheep Publishing
Findlay, Ohio

Interior Design by JW Manus
Cover Design by Valerie Lennox

To all the 4-H kids I ran around with back in the day and our advisors who put up with our shenanigans

Author's Note

The characters of Josephine "Jo" Bice, Rachel Wilson, Rose Gleeson, and James "Jimmy" Birkheimer first appeared in *Amish, Vamps & Thieves*, the fourth novel in the Bloodlines series. Rachel was pregnant with Kirsten and Kaley in that novel, making them a month older than Ellie Stephens-Howell, who will show up later in this series.

Events mentioned here such as the split of the Killbuck Pack and the Battle of Millersburg also occurred during *Amish, Vamps & Thieves*. However, the Rainier Outing, where the supernatural folks were revealed to the world happened in *Resurrected*, the ninth novel of the Bloodlines series.

I mentioned these for those interested in further knowledge of this world.

Chapter 1

When the dark cherry front door of Aunt Jo's coffee shop slammed open, Kirsten Wilson jumped. The coffee pot filled with the day's special, a fresh, hot Jamaican Blue blend, slipped from her damp hand. She watched in slow-motion horror as the glass pot dropped toward the red and white tile floor.

Instinctively, she reached out with her powers. Unfortunately, her elemental specialty was water, not earth. The pot shattered against the ceramic tiles, but the java swirled and steamed in midair. Freezing wind blew through the doorway as Rose Gleason struggled to close the coffee shop door against the mid-morning autumn storm. Aunt Jo rushed over to help the elderly lady.

Kirsten grabbed a clean, empty pot. She concentrated a bit more and shifted the hot coffee from her bubble of magick into the new pot. Thank goodness, no other customers were in the shop. Even though the existence of supernaturals had been exposed due to their efforts to save the Normals who couldn't evacuate Puget Sound when the former Mount Rainier had erupted eleven years ago, there was still a lot of suspicion and fear among the Normal community.

Not to mention, Mom and Dad always said not to show off.

Rain splattered even harder against the coffee shop's huge plate glass windows. The edges of the forest green awning over the entrance and windows danced and rippled from the storm's gusts. A few people hurried into the courthouse across the way, but no one treaded the sidewalks on this side of Jackson Street in such a blustery, wet, cold morning.

"I'm so sorry, ladies." Miz Rose panted. "Darn wind." She turned seventy last month, and from the way her fingers curled, her arthritis was getting worse. Between that, the drop in temperatures, and the fierce wind, no wonder she lost her grip on the brass door handle.

"What can we get you, Miz Rose?" Kirsten dumped the broken glass into the trash and wiped her hands on her orange apron as Jo helped their only customer out of her coat. Rose Gleason had been their 4-H Club advisor when Kirsten and her twin Kaley joined. She insisted her club members call her "Rose" because "Mrs. Gleason" was her mother-in-law. Holmes County, Ohio, was far too conservative not to have an honorific, so "Miz Rose" had stuck as her name forever.

"A cinnamon latte, please." A frown creased Miz Rose's face. "But I'm not here for just coffee."

"A Tarot card reading? A little gossip?" Jo grinned. Even though both women were the same age, the life expectancy for witches was one hundred-thirty years. Jo could have passed as Kirsten's older sister with the right hairstyle, clothes, and makeup. No gray marred Jo's mahogany braid, the same mahogany both Mom and Kirsten had. Thank goddess, Jo didn't wear elastic-waist polyester pants, but sometimes, she said something incongruous with her physical appearance.

When Kirsten's twin Kaley teased Jo about being old enough to see the first moon landing live on TV, their great aunt said the Rainier Outing was the best thing that ever happened. Otherwise, she would have had to sell her coffee shop and move to another town by now to avoid the scrutiny of Normals. And she could stop dying gray streaks in her hair.

Miz Rose toddled to her left, checking the matching cherry tables and chairs past the service counter and the hallway leading to the restrooms. There was nothing on that side of the store but the framed paintings and photos by local artists that hung on the off white walls. Once Miz Rose made sure they were alone in the coffee shop, she shuffled to a table closest to the radiator.

Kirsten started the espresso brewing while she kept an eye on their visitor. Despite Miz Rose knowing about the supernaturals long before the Outing, she and folks who were Mom's age or older still had a problem talking about woo-woo stuff in public. And if Miz Rose checked for privacy, that's exactly what she wanted to talk about.

Their elderly customer turned back to Jo. "Actually, I think I have a ghost problem." An even deeper wrinkle appeared above Miz Rose's bright orange glasses that matched her Halloween sweater. She gestured for Jo to join her before she carefully lowered herself into the wooden chair.

This month's coffee shop seat covers featured black cats and pumpkins appliqued on cream broad cloth. Mary Levy made them in addition to working the early morning shift at the coffee shop. She was currently in the back of the café putting together salads and sandwiches in preparation for lunch.

Kirsten never quite understood why the Amish community were more accepting of the supernaturals than the rest of the Normals in Millersburg. Maybe it was because they were used to being outsiders, too. Though in Mary's case, her great-great-aunt Anne had been a vampire until the cure for the disease had been discovered.

Jo took the chair beside Rose where she could keep an eye on the front door. "Sweetie—" She reached over and patted Rose's hand. "—I told you before. Your mom has passed on. She's not there."

"I don't think it's Mother." The elderly woman's eyes glistened behind her thick lenses. "I think it's Dick. Wouldn't his death count as unfinished business?"

The giant picture windows at the front of the store shivered from a harsh blast of wind. The perky scent of the espresso mixed with the warm spice of cinnamon, though neither completely blocked the sweet odor of fresh baked pastries in the well-lit glass case on the right side of the register and counter.

Kirsten listened intently to the women as she steamed the milk for Rose's latte. Rose's brother had been murdered by the Millersburg Monster before Kirsten and her twin Kaley had been born.

Except there wasn't really a monster. Just a trapped Native American water spirit forced to kill against its will. But the monster version sounded cooler, and one of the Normal farmers used the idea for his cornfield maze every year. The event drew so many people from Cleveland and Columbus it drove Sheriff Birkheimer a little crazy trying to find extra help for traffic control for the month of October.

"What makes you think it's Mister Dick?" Kirsten asked. "If he was still hanging around, wouldn't he have made himself known long before now?"

Jo pursed her lips and glared at Kirsten. She ducked her head and retrieved the can of whipped cream from the mini-refrigerator under the counter.

"Rose, maybe it's time to think about—" Jo started.

Kirsten rolled her eyes. Sometimes, her great-aunt wasn't the most subtle person on the face of the planet. Miz Rose's explosion of temper would have been expected by anybody else who dared to suggest she was too old to be living alone in a giant Victorian.

"I am not moving!" The elderly woman's frail body shook. "That house has been in my family for six generations! I am not leaving!"

Kirsten set the hot cup in front of Miz Rose. "What if I come over after the lunch rush?"

This time, both Miz Rose and Jo glared at her.

"Shouldn't you be in school?" Miz Rose said, patting her damp, iron-gray locks back in place.

"Teacher in-service day." Kirsten squared her shoulders and faced Jo. "I can check out Miz Rose's house. If there's nothing, it'll relieve your mind. And if there's something—"

"You'll come get me." Jo leaned back in her chair and crossed her arms. "The last thing we need is a ghost possessing you, young lady."

Oh, geez! Like she'd be stupid enough to let a ghost kick her out of her own body. But somehow, Kirsten squelched the urge to roll her eyes again. If she did, Jo would forbid her from going to Rose's house.

Right before Jo tattled on her to Mom.

"If there's something in Miz Rose's house, I'll come straight back here and let you know." Kirsten shut up and waited, a trick her twin never understood. She knew the I-just-turned-seventeen argument wouldn't fly with her great-aunt.

Finally, the crinkles around Jo's eyes eased, and her nostrils flared as she exhaled. "Fine. But I want you to call me before you go home, and let me know either way."

"Yes, ma'am."

Jo inclined her head toward the kitchen. "Tell Mary to take it easy on the salads. A dozen will do." She turned to watch the street. A couple of minivans rolled by, but no pedestrians. Raindrops fell sideways in the fierce wind and smacked the huge picture windows with sharp little reports. Jo shook her head. "I don't think we'll get much business with this weather."

Turned out, Jo was so very wrong on that count. Between the cold wind and spitting rain, half of Millersburg decided they wanted something hot, whether it be soup or coffee, to go with their salad or sandwich. In fact, it was nearly three before business died enough for Kirsten to clock out.

"You still going to Rose's house?" Jo eyed Kirsten.

"Yes, ma'am, I am," she answered as she slung on her burgundy waterproof jacket.

Jo inclined her head toward the back of the shop and lowered her voice. "There's some white sage sticks in my desk. Bottom drawer on the right."

"Thanks, Aunt Jo." Kirsten grinned and headed toward the storeroom cum office. Once she secured two of the sage sticks, a pack of matches, and a Ziploc bag of salt in a larger Ziploc to keep everything dry inside her backpack, she returned to the front to find Kaley leaning against the pastry display case. Her twin wore her varsity jacket and jeans.

Like cheerleaders should get to wear a varsity jacket.

"Don't get your fingerprints all over that," Kirsten snapped. "I just cleaned the glass."

"Be nice to me if you want a ride home in the rain," Kaley shot back, flipping her bottle-blond hair over her shoulder in the process. "Mom sent me to get you."

"Fine. But I have a stop first." Kirsten turned and waved. "See you Saturday morning, Jo!"

Their great-aunt waved absently before turning back to Augusta Wright who was ordering pastries for next week's Ladies Auxiliary meeting. Once they were outside, Kirsten could feel her sister's eyes on her despite them both ducking their heads against the wind and the rain.

"Where do we need to go?" Kaley yelled over the ropes slapping against the flagpole in front of the courthouse. "I've got some time before I need to be at Tina's."

Kirsten shook her head. "Babysitting again?"

Kaley shrugged. "After her ugly divorce, I don't blame her for wanting to go out for some stress relief."

Despite having a good job in the Pomerene Hospital administration department, Tina Eisler's idea of stress relief involved sleeping with every eligible male in Holmes County, plus a couple of ineligible ones. She really needed to pay more attention to her two kids, who were hurting just as bad as she was. However, Kirsten kept her mouth shut on that topic. Mom treated Tina like her little sister no matter how bad Tina screwed up at life or magick.

"What?" Kaley said as they rounded the shop and crossed the parking lot. "No smart ass comments about Tina?"

"Not today. I need to get over to the old Miller Mansion."

"Miz Rose's place? Why?"

"I just need to check out a problem she's having."

"What kind of problem?" Kaley tapped the key fob to unlock the doors of Mom's little sedan. When Kirsten remained silent after they climbed inside, Kaley waved the fob. "Spill unless you want to walk there in the rain."

Kirsten sighed. No, she didn't. It was only spitting rain now, but more gray clouds darkened the sky to the west. If she walked, she wouldn't make it to Miz Rose's house before the next wave hit.

On the other hand, she wanted to prove to both Mom and Jo she could handle things on her own. Kaley didn't take her magick studies as seriously, and their older relatives assumed her lack of focus applied to Kirsten as well. It irritated the hell out of her.

"Miz Rose thinks she has a ghost."

"Awesome!" Kaley flashed a maniacal grin before she pressed the button to start the car. "I'm coming with you if you're going to bust a ghost."

"What about Tina's kids?"

"I don't have to be there until seven." Kaley backed out of the spot. "Plenty of time."

Kirsten leaned back in the passenger seat. Part of her was annoyed by her sister tagging along. But another part was glad to have backup.

Just in case there really was a ghost haunting Miz Rose's house.

Chapter 2

The dark skeletal limbs of the oaks, maples, and ashes on the street danced in the wind when Kaley braked in front of the Miller Mansion. The light spatters turned into huge, heavy drops on their way over to Miz Rose's place. The Victorian's Federal blue painted clapboards and white gingerbread trim stood guard over the pumpkins, the cornstalks, and the riot of yellow and red mums decorating the wraparound porch.

Kaley glanced at her twin. Kirsten had been silent for the six blocks they'd driven. Not that her sister was talkative in the normal course of events.

"Is Miz Rose still on that kick about her mom haunting her?" Kaley shifted the gear into park and cut the engine.

"No." Kirsten faced her. "She thinks this thing is her brother Dick."

An icy sensation climbed Kaley's spine. "He was one of the wanagamesak's victims."

"Yeah, but all that happened a few months before we were born." Kirsten frowned. "So if it is him, why did he wait until now to make his presence known?"

The tight bun she wore while working at Jo's seemed to pull the skin around her eyes into a grimace of pain. That was part of the reason Kaley dyed her hair blond. She didn't want to look like an uptight, spinster librarian the way her sister did.

"He died at Matt Jessup's place, not here." Kaley leaned on the steering wheel and watched the Victorian. Lights gleamed through the storm's twilight from the two front rooms. "Heck, Mister Dick and his wife lived on the other side of town when he was killed. Why would his ghost come back here?"

"Both Miz Rose and Mister Dick grew up in this house," Kirsten murmured. "There might be something here his spirit's latched onto."

Kaley looked at her twin again. "You got something to cover your butt?"

Kirsten hooked her thumb inside the neck of her coffee shop t-shirt and pulled out a silver chain with a pentacle. "Protective charm. Don't leave home without it. Plus, Jo gave me some white sage and salt."

Kaley unlatched the driver's door and shoved it open. Her hand automatically slipped into the left front pocket of her jeans. Yep, her steel triquetra was still secured to the chain for her house keys. After hearing Jo and Mom's stories of the Battle of Millersburg between the fae and the Normals, it only made sense to carry something a little more utilitarian. She slammed the door shut and raced through the sharp, pelting rain up the walkway behind Kirsten.

They tore up the wide steps to the Miller Mansion's front porch. Kirsten shot her a dirty look as she wiped rain from her face.

"You could have redirected the wind a little."

Kaley grinned. "And you could have cut us a path through the rain."

Her twin rolled her eyes before she knocked on the polished mahogany door. What the hell crawled up her butt? She was acting like she didn't want Kaley here.

The door opened, and a blast of air colder than the current October storm hit Kaley in the face. Poor Miz Rose looked like she was on the verge of tears.

"Thank goodness you girls came." The sound of glass shattering came from further inside the house. "That-that thing is destroying my family photos in the sun room."

"Is it visible?" Kirsten asked.

Miz Rose shook her head. "I only knew where it was when it moved things. Moving my keepsakes is one thing." She gulped air. "But now it's destroying them!"

Kaley pressed her key fob into the older woman's palm. "Put your coat on and sit in Mom's car with the engine on so you have some heat. We'll take care of this."

"B-but—"

Kirsten grabbed Miz Rose's tan trench coat from the coat rack by the front door and shoved it into her hands. "We can protect ourselves, and we don't want you to get hurt. We'll be out once we've taken care of your problem."

A tear rolled down Miz Rose's cheek. "Be careful, girls" She donned her outerwear and walked out onto the porch, pulling the front door firmly shut behind her.

Another crash echoed through the old house. Kaley winced. Maybe Miz Rose was right about it being her brother. Only someone who died in horrible circumstances showed this kind of violence.

Kirsten dug into her backpack and pulled out her bag of supplies. "Come on."

"Maybe we should call Mom or Jo," Kaley murmured. More sounds of glass breaking came from further in the mansion.

Kirsten scowled. "If we do, you know they'll never see us as anything but incompetent. Besides, you were all gung-ho about ghost busting with me."

Dammit! Kaley hated it when Kirsten threw her own words back in her face. "Give me the sage. You take the salt."

Kirsten glanced at her, but she handed over the sage and matches.

Kaley didn't say anything more. She wasn't afraid despite the nasty look her sister gave her. She just didn't want to attract the attention of whatever was tearing apart Rose's sunroom before they were armed. It took her a second to light the first sage stick. She shoved the bag with the remaining stick and the matches into her jacket pocket.

She circled the formal parlor and the front sitting room, both filled with antiques Miz Rose's family had collected over the generations. Kirsten followed but stayed out of her way as Kaley purified each room. They continued past the grand staircase and circled the piano room and Miz Rose's office. She even purified the downstairs half bath for good measure.

The bangs and crashes intensified the closer they got to the last two rooms. They crept to the edge of the kitchen and peered around the doorway.

All of Miz Rose's cutlery, from a pair of huge meat shears to her set of good silver table knives, hung in mid-air. Each blade circulated through the room like they were living sentries.

Kaley eased back and tugged on her sister's jacket. They retreated to the back staircase.

"Did you see anything?" she said softly.

"Other than the blades of death, no," Kirsten whispered back. "So, maybe not a ghost after all."

"But Miz Rose is seventy," Kaley murmured. "It doesn't make

sense for it to be a poltergeist. Those things usually attach themselves to someone going through puberty."

Kirsten shrugged. "Maybe one of her grandkids accidentally brought it here. Give me the other sage stick."

Yet another crash reverberated through the house from the sunroom.

"Salt dissipates the nasty spirits, too," Kaley hissed.

"This is going to take both," Kirsten whispered. "And we don't have enough salt to tackle both the kitchen and the sunroom. We need to take care of the knives first and grab extra salt from Miz Rose's cupboard."

Kaley wanted to argue, but the *boom* of something heavy hitting the sunroom floor sent vibrations through the soles of her sneakers. If she and Kirsten didn't do something quick, the entity, whatever it was, would destroy Rose's house with them in it. She reluctantly pulled the Ziploc bag from her jacket pocket and handed it to Kirsten.

It took her sister several seconds to light the second sage stick. Fire seemed reluctant to exist in Kirsten's presence, like it knew she was a water witch. Finally though, the end of the stick flared into orange flames. Kirsten blew it out, and puffs of smoke curled from the end.

Kaley peeked around the corner and held out her smoldering sage. The knives quivered in midair. As tendrils of smoke wafted through the kitchen, the blades dodged the gray puffs. Kirsten dove for the other side of the doorway. A small paring knife darted toward her. Kaley clenched her fist and shot a ball of compressed air at the sharp steel, driving it down. The paring knife tumbled when it hit the hardwood floor. Thankfully, the blade didn't make any gouges on the polished planks. Probably because the knife's tip had bent from the compressed air.

She looked at Kirsten. Her sister gave a slight shake of her head, indicating she was fine. That little knife could have done some serious damage if it hit the right spot.

Kaley held up three fingers. Kirsten nodded. At the end of their silent count, both girls charged into the kitchen.

The knives split into two groups. Kaley gulped when the butcher knife aimed for her head. She mumbled the words of the necessary spell, gestured with her left hand, and pulled the smoke from her sage stick into a large light gray shield. Most of the knives clattered to the floor when they touched the purifying burnt sage cloud.

However, the butcher knife and a couple of bread slicers held back. They tried to flank her, but she hugged her back against the wall. She glanced across the kitchen.

Kirsten was in trouble. She'd grabbed a huge silver serving tray and used it to protect herself. The knives targeting her dashed in, but she couldn't concentrate the smoke enough to take out more than one at a time. There wasn't even a vase of flowers in the kitchen she could suck the water from for an offense weapon.

Kaley looked wildly around the kitchen. As if it knew what she was thinking, the butcher knife positioned itself between her and the sink. But Rose's refrigerator had a water dispenser. She aimed a compact ball of air at the lever. Water streamed out and all over the antique hardwood floor.

"Kirsten!"

Her sister reached out with her abilities and pulled the liquid into the open Ziploc full of salt.

All the knives ignored Kaley in favor of the new danger. Tendrils of salt water snapped out from behind the silver platter and neutralized knives. Kaley pushed her sage smoke shield into the whirling blades attempting to pierce her twin, and the rest tumbled to the floor.

Kirsten peered over the top of the platter. "Is that all of them?"

"Yeah, at least in here." Kaley ran over to the stove and opened the closest cabinet. Bingo! She pulled out Miz Rose's round carton of iodized salt. The container felt full. Good, they may need all of it. "You need more water?"

In response, the refrigerator dispenser hummed. She turned around.

A third tendril of water joined the other two that circled her twin. Kirsten grinned. "Pour some salt on the counter."

Once Kaley did so, the third tendril of water lapped up every grain before it returned to orbiting Kirsten. She handed her sage stick to Kaley. While they'd battled the knives, no other sounds had come from the sunroom.

"Have you seen anything?" Kirsten whispered the same question Kaley asked earlier.

She shook her head. One of the advantages of being a witch was the ability to see ghosts. But there was nothing in the kitchen that could be powering the knives. What the hell was going on here? This situation had all the makings of a vengeful spirit. Poltergeists could be mischievous and damaging, but they weren't normally this vicious. So where was the ghost? It had to be nearby.

What sounded like more glass shattering came from the sunroom. So much for their moment of quiet. Their culprit had to be hiding in there.

"We needed to get rid of the knives first," Kaley hissed. "Last thing we need is to get stabbed in the back while we deal with what's in there." She inclined her head toward the entrance to the sunroom.

The three spinning rings of water joined into one huge blob above Kirsten's head. She pantomimed opening the mudroom and having Kaley blow the cutlery out there. The action would be noisy as all get out, but it would be efficient. Kaley nodded in agreement.

Once again, they silently counted down to three. Kirsten yanked the mudroom door open. Kaley used several blasts of wind to push the knives along the floor and into the mudroom along with as much smoke from the sage sticks as she could gather. The noise was everything she expected and more when the steel blades hit the ceramic tiles lining the mudroom floor. Kirsten slammed the door shut and locked it, both manually and with a spell.

Kaley crept to the doorway to the sunroom and peered around the jamb. The heat of Kirsten's body penetrated the back of her varsity jacket.

Cracks marred the huge Florida windows where objects had struck them, but the double-paned glass still held together. The last painted plaster handprint hanging on the north wall rattled before it jerked loose, pulling its brass hanger and a huge chunk of drywall with it. The child's artwork darted through the air and hit the fireplace. The shattered plaster joined the other three smashed pieces on the hearth.

None of the family photographs that adorned the walls and shelves remained intact. Glass shards and broken frames littered the carpet. The photos themselves looked as if someone had taken a jagged piece of broken glass, or one of the knives currently locked in the mudroom, and scored the pictures. The pillows and cushions previously on the couches and chairs had been disemboweled. White fluffs spilled out of the multitude of slashes inflicted on the various fabrics, and a large number of puffs lay amid the glass shards.

No wonder Miz Rose was in tears when they arrived. She and her part-time housekeeper kept the rest of the family Victorian immaculate. It was on the National Historic Register after all. But this was the room she lived in every day. Not to mention how much she cherished her grandchildren. Their school photographs she had proudly displayed were now in tatters all over her carpet.

Something pale blue and transparent drifted across the sunroom. It was roughly the size of a young child, but its edges were fragmented and wispy. A feeling of malevolence came from it.

A specter. Most ghosts retained enough of their humanity that they could be reasoned with. Specters, however, had gone mad by staying in this plane of existence as an incorporeal entity for too long. They were the ultimate in passive-aggressive sociopaths. Not to mention, a total bitch to get rid of.

Was this one trying to set up in the Miller Mansion by driving out Miz Rose? Her home was one of the oldest buildings in Millersburg, if not the entire state of Ohio.

You sure we're not out of our depths here? she said silently to Kirsten. There had been a time when the only way she and her sister spoke to each other was telepathically. Dad had been the one who pointed out how rude it was in front of Normals like him. It hadn't really stopped them, but since they started high school, they seemed to be drifting apart. Kaley hated it, but every time she tried to talk to Kirsten about it, her sister snapped that she was tired of living in Kaley's shadow. Why was it Kaley's fault she got along better with people than Kirsten did?

You decided to tag along, Kirsten said.

It's a good thing, too, Kaley shot back.

A wave of annoyance came from her twin. Kaley wanted to curse the freaking chip her sister carried on her shoulder. Kirsten was the one who wanted to carve her own space, but any time Kaley did that for herself, Kirsten got her panties in a wad about it. But darn it, they didn't have to do the same thing all the time.

Can you please focus on the problem instead of trying to one-up me? Kirsten snapped.

Fine. I'll shield us. You zap anything that comes our way, Kaley said. She let a thread of her own irritation wash through their mental link.

Kirsten grimaced, but she nodded in agreement to the plan.

Ignoring her twin's pissy attitude, Kaley passed the second sage stick to her right hand. With her free left hand, she reached out with her powers and pulled the smoke in a light gray circle roughly four feet in diameter. She clenched her fist as if she were holding a solid material shield.

The specter shrieked, the nails-on-blackboard sound painful to Kaley's ears. Glass shards rose into the air, quivering like the knives in the kitchen had. The jagged, glittering pieces darted for her and her sister.

Kaley's shield held off most of the first wave. The glass dropped to the thick carpet with soft thuds as the sage smoke purified the bits. Kirsten's saltwater tendrils zapped the slivers that tried to go around Kaley's smoke shield.

Another shriek from the specter split the air an instant before Miz Rose's flat screen flew across the room. Kaley's shield couldn't stop the TV's sheer momentum. She shoved Kirsten onto the slashed up loveseat and landed on top of her as the device sailed past them. Sounds of glass and plastic smashing onto the hardwood floor came from the kitchen.

Kaley pulled her sage smoke shield into a half-sphere around herself and Kirsten, and she reinforced it with the whispered spell of a ward. Plaster and ceramic fragments and the remnants of metal and wood frames pounded against her magick.

Kirsten squirmed from beneath her and rolled off the couch and out of Kaley's ward.

"What are you—" Kaley yelled.

Her twin's tendrils of saltwater shot out and wrapped themselves around the specter. This time, its shriek sounded like one of pain instead of fury. It fizzled into blue smoke and disappeared.

Kaley released the ward and the smoke shield. She panted from the adrenaline rush still firing through her nervous system. Her heart pounded. The scent of plastic burning stung her nose. The smoldering sage sticks had ignited a hunk of polyester pillow filling.

She snatched the hunk of fluff, rolled to her feet, and created a vacuum around the tips of her index finger and thumb. The fire and melted section of polyester winked out until only black gunk coated that end of the filling. She took it over to the fireplace and laid it on the hearth before she turned back to Kirsten.

"You okay?" Kaley asked.

"I'm not trying to set Miz Rose's house on fire." Kirsten smirked. "Where'd it go? We sure didn't banish it."

Blue smoke formed behind Kirsten.

"Behind you!"

But Kirsten was already ducking and pivoting as Kaley shouted her warning. Saltwater tendrils lashed for the specter. It separated before the purifying water hit it, and it flowed to another spot to reform.

Kaley pulled the sage smoke back to herself. "Drive it toward the fireplace!"

The specter waved an amorphous blue limb in her direction. The fireplace poker rose and launched itself at her. Like the TV, she couldn't stop the poker's momentum with smoke. The glass-covered carpet would do less damage than the projectile would.

She dove for the floor. Shards stabbed her in the thighs and forearms. The steel knocked off a huge chuck of plaster, but it couldn't penetrate the original brick of the house. The poker landed with a thud.

Kirsten waved her hands. The tendrils of saltwater divided themselves into hundreds of threads. She wove them into a tighter net around the specter and drove it toward the fireplace. With one last shriek of rage, it flowed up the flue.

Kaley held the sage sticks above her head to keep from setting anything else on fire and pushed herself upright with one hand. Kirsten turned toward Kaley, and her eyes widened.

"You're bleeding!"

"It's better than getting brained by a poker," Kaley said dryly. She looked at the fireplace. "But I'm beginning to think whatever that thing was, it wasn't a specter either."

"So what the hell were we fighting?"

Kaley looked at her sister. "I hate to say this, but we might want to hit the books when we get home."

Chapter 3

Kirsten retrieved Miz Rose from Mom's car. The elderly woman clucked her tongue while she examined the bloody slices on Kaley's arms and legs. Luckily, her varsity jacket and heavy jeans saved her from the worst of the damage, and none of the cuts on her hands were deep enough to need stitches.

Once they bandaged Kaley's wounds, Kirsten couldn't leave Miz Rose alone to clean up the mess in her house. She suggested Kaley cleanse and purify the second and third floors with the white sage smoke as well as the basement while she picked up glass and plaster in the sunroom and retrieved the knives from the mudroom. For once, Kaley didn't argue with her.

It took them over an hour before Kirsten was satisfied she'd vacuumed all the shards out of the carpet and upholstery in the sunroom. Kaley pulled Kirsten aside after she put away Miz Rose's upright in the closet beneath the back staircase.

"What are you planning to do to keep that thing from coming back?" Kaley whispered.

"If it wasn't raining like crazy, I'd say a salt circle." Kirsten shrugged. She hated asking for help, but her pride wasn't worth Miz Rose's safety. "I'm open to suggestions."

For the second time today, Kaley didn't make some kind of smart ass comment. "Do you have any dragon's blood on you?"

Kirsten shook her head. She should have come more prepared, but after the false alarms concerning Miz Rose's mother, she hadn't really taken the possibility of an entity haunting the poor lady more seriously.

Lesson learned.

"Let's raid her spice cupboard," Kaley said. "We should be able to find something."

"Cumin mixed with salt would be best." Kirsten sagged a bit as her brain finally kicked into gear. "Clove, more sage, thyme, rosemary—"

"Thyme and rosemary-infused vinegar works for a few days if she doesn't have any cumin," Kaley said. "At least until the vinegar evaporates."

"And here, I didn't think you were listening to Jo." Kirsten whirled and strode toward the kitchen.

Kaley followed her. "It's only a stop gap. We need to figure out why a specter's after Miz Rose."

It didn't take long for them to mix up the protection potion with the ingredients Miz Rose had on hand. They set bowls of the vinegar mixtures in every room. Luckily, Miz Rose hadn't replaced her beloved cat who'd passed away shortly before her mother. Nothing should disturb the bowls for the next day while Kirsten researched a more permanent solution.

The rain had paused when they left Miz Rose's with the excuse Mom expected them for dinner. Kirsten dropped into the passenger seat, slammed the door shut, and turned to her twin.

"Where the hell did that thing come from?"

"You're the magick geek," Kaley pursed her mouth before she punched the ignition button.

"We didn't blow up ourselves or Rose's house, so it wasn't a fae specter." Unless both practitioners were highly experienced, mixing witch and fae usually resulted in a spectacular explosion, which was why the two groups generally avoided one another.

Kirsten racked her brain. None of this made sense. "It acted more like a poltergeist. If Miz Rose is right, it didn't try to hurt anyone until you and I came into the house. But where did it come from, and why now? And why attack us?"

"Halloween is in two weeks." Kaley looked over her shoulder to check for traffic. "That would account for the now. Maybe it attacked us because it knew we could stop it."

"We still don't know why it focused on Miz Rose," Kirsten said. "She's as Normal as they come."

"It scares me when you don't know." Kaley pulled out onto the street. Traffic was practically non-existent. No one wanted to be outside on a day like this. "Consult Jo's Book of Shadows?"

"She wanted me to report back no matter what I found—" Kirsten started.

"We found," Kaley corrected as she accelerated down the street.

Irritation prickled along Kirsten's skin. "We don't have to do every single thing together."

"Really? You think I want to be little-miss-super-jock-slash-book-worm like you?"

"A basketball or educational scholarship is a lot more useful than homecoming queen on a resumé," Kirsten snapped.

"You think I can't get a scholarship?" Kaley's head whipped around so she could give Kirsten a quick dirty look. She flipped the right turn signal as she braked for the stop sign.

"I think you're not trying." Kirsten huffed. If they weren't identical, she'd wonder if someone had exchanged her sister with another baby when they were born. "Don't you want to leave this pissant town?"

"What's wrong with Millersburg?" Kaley guided the car around the corner.

"There's nothing to do here!" Kirsten gestured at the surrounding houses. Most of them were late nineteenth or early twentieth century style homes. A few Queen Annes were scattered among western bungalows and American foursquares with the occasional ranch or shotgun house.

A sharp bark of laughter erupted from Kaley. "Yes, there is. You just refuse to do it."

"Drinking while camping in the woods is not my idea of a good time" Kirsten grumbled.

"I don't drink."

Kirsten Looked at her sister. Nope, her aura remained a sparkling lemon yellow. She wasn't lying.

"Then why do you come in smelling like a keg has been dumped on you nearly every Saturday night?"

Kaley grimaced. "Because I'm usually trying to stop Donny from drinking. He *is* someone who can't afford to lose his athletic scholarship."

Of course. Donny Fryer, the smallest boy on the West Holmes football team. The local conference commission forced him to be the field goal kicker once word got out that his daddy was a werecoyote. The compromise to keep him on the team and therefore in school made his mom and the coach happy, but it gnawed on Donny's ego.

And that was the least of the kid's problems.

The Killbuck pack didn't want a damn thing to do with Donny after his daddy dragged the 'coyotes into a feud between the vampires and the fae. Worse, when they did pay attention to Donny, it was to pick on him because Kyle Warner's ex-wife was the one who ripped out his daddy's throat.

"You can't save Donny from himself," Kirsten said softly.

"It's not his fault his dad got himself killed by kidnapping another were's pups," Kaley replied.

Kirsten grimaced but kept silent. She never really understood her sister's defense of the werecoyote. The Killbuck pack split seventeen years ago over Chad Fryer, Kyle Warner, and the Abbot boys siding with the Unseelie. Or let themselves be used by the Unseelie, depending on who you talked to. Any of the 'coyotes remaining in Killbuck were just plain trouble in her eyes.

Kaley made a second right onto Jackson Street. Traffic picked up as people headed home from work. Not that there was much of a rush hour in Millersburg. It took seven to eight minutes to get across town instead of five. She pulled up in front of the coffee shop as the neon "Open" sign flicked off.

The brief pause in precipitation was over the minute Kaley killed the engine. Rain poured down the windshield in sheets.

"You going to cover our asses?" She scowled at Kirsten.

Kirsten grinned. "Yep. I don't feel like getting drenched tonight either."

Once again, they silently counted to three before they pushed their respective doors open, jumped out, and raced for the front of the shop. Kirsten concentrated and used her abilities to divert most of the rain from them, but she let a few drops get through just in case someone was watching from another building.

The front door whipped open, seemingly on its own accord.

Kirsten ran inside, Kaley on her heels. Jo pushed the door shut behind them.

"They just arrived," Jo said into her cell phone. She held it to her ear with her free hand. "I'll tell her, and I'll bring Kirsten home." She lowered the device and thumbed a control. "Your mother's been trying to get a hold of you two for the past couple of hours. And Kaley, Tina needs you at her house at six, not seven. She's been trying to call you, too."

Kirsten looked at her sister. She was pretty sure she had the same confused expression as her twin. They both pulled their phones out of their pockets.

"No voice messages and no texts," Kirsten muttered.

"Me neither," Kaley said. "You think it was the specter?"

"Specter?" Jo said.

Kirsten looked up as she shoved her phone back in her pocket. "That doesn't explain why nothing came through after all the excitement at Miz Rose's."

"Wait," Jo demanded. "Go back. What specter?"

Kirsten shrugged. "It definitely wasn't a ghost at Miz Rose's house." She used her right hand to indicate its height. "About the size of an eight-year-old kid, pale blue, indistinct, and violent as hell toward witches."

Jo's eyes widened, and color drained from her face. "What do you mean violent?"

Kaley held up her forearms, showing the bandages and the various slashes in the leather sleeves of her varsity jacket. Her irritation pricked against Kirsten's mental shields.

"We escaped Miz Rose's knives in her kitchen, but not the broken glass in her sunroom," Kaley said sourly. "Well, I didn't anyway. Dad's going to have a fit when he sees my jacket."

"Knives?" Jo stalked toward the counter. "I'll make us some tea, and you two need to start from when you arrived at Rose's house."

Once everyone had a cup of orange tea and were seated around one of the back tables, Kirsten laid out everything that happened. Kaley only interrupted to clarify a detail or add her observation. Otherwise, she let Kirsten spin the tale, which wasn't like her at all. She was the talkative sister of the two of them.

When Kirsten finished, Jo stared at the cinnamon broom hanging over the shop's main door. This broom was nothing like the ones found in the home improvement or arts and crafts stores this time of year. Jo had carefully constructed the hazel handle and tied the birch twigs with green and white string. The purposes of its materials and colors were protection of the people and contents of the shop and attraction of business.

"I need to think about this," Jo finally said. "Kirsten, check Grandma Charlie's Book of Shadows concerning specters tonight and your mom's. I'll check mine."

"Could someone have sent the specter to Miz Rose's house?" Kirsten said.

"If it had hurt Rose, I'd say yes." Jo grimaced. "Except this one only destroyed property until you girls arrived."

"Who would have assumed we'd be the ones to go to her house?" Kaley asked. "If Miz Rose asked for a witch to come over, it would have been you."

Jo's right eyebrow rose. "Exactly. Be extra careful at Tina's tonight."

Outside the huge windows, the sun had set, and the wind continued to howl. It whistled across the shop's gutters, the high-pitched screech reminiscent of the specter's angry cries. Kirsten shivered.

She sent a silent prayer to the Goddess that the potion she and Kaley had whipped together protected Miz Rose through the night. She'd never forgive herself if something happened to the elderly Normal.

Chapter 4

Kaley pulled into Tina's driveway at five minutes before six and parked next to the older teal PT Cruiser sitting on the asphalt. Orange and purple lights decorated the two apple saplings planted in front of the double-wide mobile home. Three scarecrows with jack o' lanterns as heads and dressed like Tina and her kids sat on square bales of straw between the two trees.

Thankfully, the rain had stopped for the moment. As Kaley climbed out of Mom's sedan, Tina rushed out the front door, pulling on her tan wool peacoat.

"Thank you so much for coming early," Tina said. Her black-dyed short hair stood up in spikes thanks to copious amounts of styling gel. Huge silver hoops dangled from both ears, and a single stud in the shape of a bulldog glittered above the hoop in her right ear. She wore black jeans and a purple silk button-down shirt with heels. Somehow, she managed to pull off classy and trashy at the same time.

"Is everything okay?" Kaley strode toward the older witch.

"Yeah, Jerry's truck broke down," Tina said as she jogged down the steps from the tiny stained redwood porch gracing her home. "I need to pick him up at work."

Jerry Woodham's ancient pickup may have broken down, but more likely, he'd run out of gas after spending all his money on alcohol and pot. Kaley bit the side of her cheek. No sense saying anything to Tina. She'd only get defensive over her latest boyfriend.

Tina hugged Kaley. When they parted, Tina's silver earrings reflected the Halloween lights. She'd given up the eyebrow and nose rings after Noah thought they were excellent pull toys when he was a baby.

"Pizza is already here." Tina searched through her Vera Bradley knock-off purse, obviously looking for her car keys. "The kids can make popcorn for a snack, but the Pop-Tarts are off limits if they want breakfast in the morning. And they need to leave Agatha alone. She's been pissy all day, probably because of the weather, and is currently hiding under my bed." Tina pulled out the string of keyrings topped by a rabbit's foot with its fur dyed purple.

"Got it." Kaley grinned, imagining the black feline and her moods. She was glad her own Penn was a much more gregarious cat. "Anything else?"

"No staying up past nine," Tina said firmly. "Tomorrow's a school day. And absolutely no horror movies." She relaxed a bit. "Your money's on the kitchen counter." She hugged Kaley again. "Thank you so much for coming early."

"No problem. Have fun tonight!"

Tina darted to the driver's side of her Cruiser and waved.

Kaley waved back. The Cruiser backed out of the drive and sped off down the county road. Tina was in such a hurry, she didn't even notice the slices on Kaley's coat and jeans. As she turned to enter the house, a flash of blue light in the woods across the road made her hesitate on the first step.

She faced the woods, squinted, and Looked. Nothing met either her regular eyesight or her Second Sight. Maybe she was imagining things after the craziness at Miz Rose's house this afternoon. But as Kirsten said, the specter hadn't acted against a person until she and her sister tried to put a stop to its antics. The cuts on her hands and shins reminded her of how dangerous the specter could be, and if it was deliberately targeting witches as Jo feared, then maybe Kaley needed to take some precautions. Her charges for the evening were witches themselves.

Kaley kept looking over her shoulder as she slowly climbed the steps, but no blue light showed itself again. Maybe she was imagining things after what happened at Miz Rose's. She entered the mobile home.

"Kaley!" Mila jumped up from the couch and rushed over to hug her. The child had lovely light brown curls that made her look younger than her eight years.

"Hey, Mila." Kaley smiled at her charge. "Where's your brother?"

"Sleeping." Mila shrugged. "Mom says he's getting ready for a growth spurt."

As if the twelve-year-old heard them, Noah shuffled into the living room. "Hey, Kaley. Did Mom leave already?"

"You just missed her," Kaley said brightly. An impulse grabbed her, and she blurted, "Have you two seen any lights in the woods across the road?"

Mila whirled to face Noah. "Told you I saw something!"

He grimaced at his sister. "You still see monsters under your bed."

"Monsters are real!" Mila stamped her pink-socked right foot for emphasis. "Everybody knows about them now."

Noah rolled his eyes before he shuffled to the kitchen. "I smell pizza."

Kaley ignored him as she pulled off her coat. "What did you see, Mila?" She hung her varsity jacket on a black metal peg of the farmhouse coat rack mounted on the wall before she faced the little girl.

"A blue light and it was kind of shaped like a person," Mila said with a firm nod. "Mom said not to chase it. That it might be a fairy trick."

"Your mom's right." Kaley smiled at the girl. "Did she see the blue light?"

"Nope." Mila shook her head vigorously to emphasize her answer. "Can we have pizza now? Mom said we had to wait until you got here, and we had to share."

"Sure, I'm hungry, too." Kaley followed Mila into the tiny kitchen, but she refrained from skipping like the little girl.

She retrieved clean plates from the dishwasher. Noah had already opened the box and was munching on a slice. Kaley looked into napkin holder. Empty. She set the plates on the counter and pulled open the pantry door.

"If you're looking for the napkins, we're out," Mila offered. She reached up for the roll of paper towels hanging beneath the cupboard closest to the sink and tore off a sheet. "We need to use these."

"Okay." Kirsten didn't comment on the nearly bare pantry. Besides the box of Pop-Tarts, there was a box of spaghetti, a jar of spaghetti sauce, and not much else. Tina may throw a fit, but Mom needed to know what was going on here. There were times when money had been tight in the Wilson household, but Mom and Dad always made sure there was food in the house.

She accepted the paper towel from Mila, who tore off two more sheets before she picked out her slice of pizza. Kaley selected her slice and turned to find Noah staring at them empty-handed.

"Ready for another slice?"

He grunted what sounded like an affirmative, but he waited

until Mila and Kaley stepped out of the kitchen before he went in to grab more pizza. Puberty had bitten Noah hard. Kaley almost felt sorry for Tina. Things had been rough enough for her lately. Her son copping a preteen attitude wouldn't help one bit.

Once the three of them settled on the couch, Kaley snatched the remote from the coffee table. While Noah demanded a Marvel movie and Mila pleaded for another show on the Disney channel, Kaley settled their moot argument by switching to a family-friendly game show on one of the satellite channels. Soon, the kids forgot their rivalry and teamed up to beat her and the contestants' answers to trivia questions.

Once Noah and Mila were in bed, only a few minutes later than their mom said, Kaley searched Tina's spice shelves for powdered cumin. She smiled to herself when she found a tin with the correct label. The grocery store only had the seed variety when she stopped on the way here. At least, she wouldn't have to grind the seeds.

The double-wide had the naturally-occurring wards of any dwelling, plus Tina's magick, meager as it was. Unfortunately, the trailer was still on wheels, which meant the warding wasn't as strong as a house with a foundation. It was a good thing she'd stopped at IGA's on the way to Tina's place.

After grabbing the canister of salt out of her backpack she'd picked up at the grocery, she retrieved a bowl from the dishwasher. She started to close the machine but lowered the door. If she were going to use Tina's powdered cumin, she needed to return the favor. It only took a couple of minutes to empty the clean dishes, pots, and utensils from the dishwasher and put them away, keeping out a spoon.

At a soft meow, Kaley looked down. Agatha slunk into the kitchen now that the kids were in bed, and they wouldn't insist on petting her. Leave it to Tina to have a black cat as her familiar.

"Good evening, my dear," Kaley said.

Agatha rubbed back and forth against Kaley's jeans while she poured salt into the bowl and added a couple of teaspoons of powdered cumin. While she stirred the mixture, Agatha began to purr in time to Kaley's whispered spell. Yellow energy flowed from her skin into the bowl to join with Agatha's green familiar protective energy. When the salt and cumin were properly infused with magick, Kaley considered her options.

Though the rain had stopped, the ground was pretty saturated. The salt would dissolve within minutes. She looked down at Agatha.

"Can I trust you to stay out of the spice and salt?"

Agatha cocked her head as if to say, "Do I look that stupid?"

"Sorry, I didn't mean to insult you."

The cat sniffed, stretched out her front legs, and flicked her tail before she sauntered out of the kitchen. Kaley carefully sprinkled her mixture along the kitchen floor's backsplashes. She continued around the living room, sprinkling the salt and cumin along the baseboards, then down the hallway doing the same. The bathroom was a concern since the humidity of everyone taking showers could dissolve the salt, but it would hold for tonight. She'd have to tell Tina what was going on when she got back from her date so she didn't get mad at the kids.

Both Noah and Mila were sound asleep when Kaley entered their rooms. Luckily, their mom made them pick up their stuff, so Kaley didn't trip over any toys or clothes while she distributed her mixture. Agatha supervised from the doorways.

Tina's bedroom was another story when Kaley flipped on the lights. It looked like she'd tried on several nicer outfits for her date, only to return to the jeans and blouse when Jerry called about his truck. At least, the rejected outfits were on the bed. Tina's scrubs hadn't made it to the hamper for the last couple of days. Agatha jumped up on the mattress and deliberately flopped on the nicer clothes.

Kaley set the bowl on Tina's dresser and picked up the dirty clothes before she spread the salt and cumin along the baseboard of the master bedroom under the cat's careful observation. Out of nowhere, Agatha yowled, leapt from the bed, and dived beneath the frame.

Kaley lifted the dust ruffle and ducked her head. "What's wrong, Agatha?"

The black cat hissed and swatted at Kaley.

That was weird, but Mom also said to listen to a familiar, even one that wasn't yours. Kaley tensed and climbed to her feet. Tina's bedroom curtains were still open. A flicker of blue light flashed in her peripheral vision.

Easing over to the window, Kaley peered outside. A pale blue, indistinct figure stood amid the broken stalks at the edge of the cornfield next door. She laid the bowl on the nightstand and reached into her right pocket for her own keyring. The steel triquetra was reassuring in her grip.

She didn't sense any emotion from the specter. It drifted back and forth along the border of the cornfield and Tina's yard for a minute or two before it floated back across the county road and disappeared into the woods.

Kaley released the breath she hadn't realized she'd been

holding. Now, what the hell was this thing doing all the way out at Tina's place? Was it following her after she and Kirsten had driven it out of Miz Rose's house this afternoon?

With a shaky hand, Kaley let go of her key ring and removed her hand from her right pocket. She pulled her phone out of her left pocket and thumbed the speed dial for Kirsten.

"Hello?"

"Hey, sis!" Kaley tried not to let her voice quiver. "How's the research going?"

"What happened?" Alarm filled Kirsten's tone.

"The specter showed up here." Kaley grabbed the bowl and walked toward the door.

"What? Are you okay?"

Kaley flipped off the lights. Part of her didn't want to, but the specter had attacked them during the day. Lights weren't going to make a difference.

"I'm fine," she answered. "I spread salt and cumin along the walls after I got a glimpse of it in the woods when I first got here."

"What did Noah and Mila say when they saw it tonight?"

"They didn't see it. I waited until they went to bed before I mixed the potion and cast the protection spell." Kaley headed back down the short hallway. A black blur streaked past her shoes. Obviously, Agatha didn't want to be left alone in a dark bedroom. "But I did ask them about it when I arrived. Mila admitted she's seen it before. She perfectly described the same thing we saw at Miz Rose's. A few minutes ago, it was standing in the cornfield as I finished up the protection spell in Tina's bedroom. I don't think it could enter the trailer. It seemed to pace along the property line between the Eislers' lot and Old Man Chalmers' cornfield before it drifted back into the woods."

"Do I need to—" Kirsten started when in the background,

Mom shouted, "What's this about you and your sister almost getting stabbed by a specter?"

Kirsten's sigh whistled through the receiver. "Let me call you back in a minute."

Well, crap. Kaley exhaled. Mom's lectures were never short, and she'd get her share when she got home. In the meantime, what was she supposed to do if the specter managed to break her protection spell on the trailer?

Chapter 5

Kirsten grimaced as Mom charged into her bedroom, a furious expression on her face. Mom's shouting had woken Penn and Teller, who lay next to Kirsten on her deep purple comforter. The two tabby cats raised their heads, looked at Mom and Kirsten, and decided it wasn't an emergency. They stretched and sprawled, no doubt planning on going back to sleep.

Kirsten thumbed the icon to end Kaley's call and sat up to face the consequences of this afternoon's misadventure. "It wasn't as bad as whatever Jo told you."

"Jo?" Mom's eyes widened. "She knew about this?" Rachel Wilson may have been one of the most beautiful women in Holmes County, but few people crossed her, even before they knew she was a witch. Between her temper and her position as editor-in-chief of the *Millersburg Monitor*, people had found themselves publicly shamed for whatever crime Mom deemed them guilty of committing. According to rumors, she'd even given the vampires' goddess of death a tongue lashing once.

Crap. Kirsten set her phone on her nightstand. She shouldn't have made an assumption and thrown Jo under the proverbial bus. Unfortunately, her action drew Mom's eyes to the grimoire she'd been reading.

"What are you doing with my mother's Book of Shadows?" Mom said, her voice low and dangerous.

That woke up both cats again. Teller gave an inquiring meow, but Kirsten ignored her familiar. The gray tabby curled up against his golden brother, but his eyes remained open.

Kirsten sucked in a deep breath. "Miz Rose thought it was the ghost of her older brother haunting her house. All we were—"

"We?" Mom crossed her arms. "Your sister is involved in this, too?"

Double crap. Kaley would kill her if Jo didn't first. And Kirsten couldn't blame her twin one bit. She would be pissed if their positions were reversed.

"I was just supposed to check out the situation since I got off work before Jo." Kirsten raised her hands, fingers spread wide. "Jo said to report back to her about what we found, and we did. Kaley was only supposed to drop me off at Miz Rose's." Her shoulders sagged. "I'm glad she stuck around because it wasn't a ghost, and I needed the help. Now, the specter's followed her over to Tina's place."

Mom muttered a few words Kirsten didn't think were in her vocabulary. "Grab your coat. You and Jo are coming with me to get your sister."

"But she laid down a protective spell on the doublewide using salt and cumin," Kirsten protested.

"And what's going to cover her ass once she leaves Tina's trailer?" Mom shook her head sadly. "Ethan needs to get that '69 Buick running for you girls. That has enough iron to protect you from the fae. And no more exchanging the silver jewelry my family gives you as gifts!"

Kirsten swallowed hard. The disappointment in Mom's voice tore at her. Kaley was the one who preferred gold and exchanged her presents, not her. But even if Dad got the '69 working, she and Kaley may never be allowed to leave the house again.

"We weren't careless—" she started.

"No, you lied to me by omission," Mom snapped.

Kirsten swung her legs off her bed and leapt to her feet. "Should we have let that thing kill Miz Rose? It was already terrorizing her!"

A shocked expression appeared on Mom's face. Kirsten was sure she had the same look on hers. Kaley was the one who talked back to their parents. Kirsten couldn't lie to herself about where her anger came from.

"Look, I know you're trying to protect us, but Kaley and I both need to practice our gifts." Kirsten crossed her arms and matched Mom's stance. "What do you think is going to happen a century down the road when you and Jo are gone? How are Kaley and I supposed to protect your grandchildren and great-grandchildren if we don't know how?"

Mom finally relaxed, and a wan smile tilted her mouth. "You're right." She took a deep breath and released it. "How bad were the cuts?"

"I'm fine. Kaley's jacket and jeans took the brunt. Trust me, she didn't need any stitches." Kirsten considered her options before she admitted, "It was either landing on the broken glass or take a fireplace poker through her skull. She made the right choice, and we managed to drive that thing out of Miz Rose's house."

Mom's mouth opened, then closed. Finally, she pursed her lips before she said, "You purified the entire house afterward?"

Kirsten nodded. "Attic to basement."

"Have you figured out where the specter came from?"

Kirsten waved at her grandmother's Book of Shadows. "No. That's why I was researching. It started off with poltergeist-level pranks that gradually grew worse. According to Rose, it didn't become deadly until we showed up this afternoon. We thought it was a specter, considering the level of violence, but its behavior isn't matching anything in the Book"

"I'll probably have to make some phone calls if Mother doesn't have anything listed." Mom sighed. "Let's not tell your dad about this."

"Really, Mom?" Kirsten tilted her head and tried to hide her amusement. "Lying by omission?"

"You know he'll react worse than me if he finds out." Mom sniffed.

"It's going to be hard to hide it when he sees the cuts on Kaley's jacket," Kirsten pointed out.

"Fine," Mom grudgingly admitted. "We'll tell him in the morning. I'm not waking him up tonight for this. And you're right. He's going to notice the salt and cumin around the house." She stared up at the ceiling and shook her head. "Why on earth did I fall in love with a Normal?"

Kirsten grinned. "Because you liked how his ass looked in jeans." It was the common refrain Jo said every time Mom asked the same question.

"Go get your coat, young lady, before I change my mind about corporal punishment." But there was a touch of humor in Mom's reprimand.

Mom drove to Aunt Jo's house in Dad's white pickup with his veterinarian office's name and address stenciled on the doors. After Jo climbed in the front passenger seat of the cab, Mom spent the ride over to Tina's blasting their aunt for getting Kirsten and Kaley involved with an unknown entity.

Kirsten stared at the asphalt illuminated by the truck's headlights. This late at night, there weren't any cars on the township road Mom took. No moon tonight either. No wonder Kaley had gotten a good look at the specter while it was in the cornfield.

"This alleged specter isn't acting like anything described in Grandma Charlie's Book of Shadows," Kirsten interjected when both Mom and Jo paused their arguing to take a breath. "Could someone be controlling it?"

Mom and Jo exchanged worried looks.

"The last time someone controlled a spirit in Millersburg—" Mom began.

"The girls would have blown up themselves and Rose if this thing was fae related," Jo said.

"First of all, Kaley gave Miz Rose her protection charm, and we sent her out to Mom's sedan for her own safety," Kirsten pointed out. "Second, Kaley and I already figured out it wasn't fae related when it tried to stab us with Miz Rose's entire collection of kitchen knives. That could mean someone's using a magickal object, or it could be another witch."

The two older women remained quiet as they considered her words.

"The only witches in town are us, Tina, and her kids," Jo said.

"Unless it's a tourist messing with us," Mom replied.

"Why would an outside witch target a local witch?" Kirsten asked.

"There's only our exes we have any beef with," Jo murmured. It wasn't often Jo mentioned hers or Mom's first husbands.

"What if Rose is the target?" Mom said. "She worked for Fitz until he was Turned. And vampires have very long memories."

Colin Fitzgerald, Miz Rose's old boss, was a Normal attorney, but he'd fallen in love with Mary's great-great-aunt Anne. He willingly allowed himself to be infected with the virus that caused vampirism in order to spend the rest of his life with her. It may have sounded terribly romantic, but there were huge costs in becoming a vampire, especially in choosing which coven to join. Since Anne belonged to the St. James Coven, that's the one Mr. Fitzgerald joined. They lived in Los Angeles these days. However, Ohio was under the control of the Dare Coven.

To say Virginia Dare didn't like Duncan St. James was an understatement.

"If Master Dare wanted to torture Miz Rose, she'd make sure Mr. Fitzgerald knew about it," Kirsten said.

Both Mom and Jo shot surprised looks at her.

"I pay attention to your supernatural civics lectures," Kirsten said. "Stop equating me with Kaley."

Mom sighed and returned her attention to the road. "I'm sorry, sweetie. I didn't mean—"

A whitetail doe darted from the left across the road. Mom slammed on the brakes. Kirsten's seatbelt prevented her from being flung into the front seat of the pickup.

"You two okay?" Mom said.

Both Kirsten and Jo murmured affirmatives. A few seconds later, the rest of the herd charged across the asphalt after the first deer and disappeared over the embankment on the right.

"What's got the deer spooked?" Jo said.

Kirsten looked over her shoulder and out the back window of the pickup. A glowing pale blue figure floated toward them. "I'd say it's the specter right behind us."

Mom pressed the accelerator. The pickup's tires squealed before they grabbed the blacktop. The force slammed Kirsten against the back of the bench seat, and the truck roared down the narrow township road.

Chapter 6

Kaley flipped through one of Tina's celebrity gossip magazines as she waited for Tina to get home. After Mom interrupted her conversation with Kirsten, Kaley had gone through the doublewide and closed all the blinds and curtains, including the ones in the kids' bedrooms. Last thing she needed was the specter peering in the windows and scaring the bejeezus out of her charges.

When she entered Noah's room, he had been sleeping on top of his covers, but his red and black plaid sleep pants and black long-sleeved t-shirt seemed to be keeping him warm enough. He blearily raised his head and asked what was going on. Kaley made some excuse about him sleeping better with no outside light. He wasn't awake enough to question her bullcrap and was snoring before she closed the bedroom door behind her.

Her phone rang as she walked back down the hallway, and she checked the caller ID. Kirsten.

She tapped the Answer icon. "Is Mom—" In the background, tires screeched.

"Shut up and listen." Fear flavored Kirsten's tone. "Mom insisted we come get you. We're in Dad's truck, and that damn specter is chasing us."

"Go home!" Kaley's heart pounded. "The kids and I are safe—"

"Tina's place is closer than our house," Kirsten said. "We'll be there in a minute or two. Stand by the front door with extra cumin and salt."

Kaley was up and headed for the kitchen before her sister finished speaking. "There's enough steel in Dad's pickup to protect you—"

"This thing isn't acting like the specters described in Grandma Charlie's Book of Shadows—Hey!"

"Kaley, are the kids safe?" Jo's voice came through the receiver. She must have grabbed Kirsten's phone out of her hand.

Kaley tapped the speaker function and set the phone on the counter next to the bowl she'd used earlier. Part of her was a little glad she hadn't loaded it and the spoon into the dishwasher yet, and she'd left out the salt and cumin just in case. "Yeah, I salted the whole trailer, and I closed their blinds and curtains a little bit ago when I checked on them."

She dumped more salt into the bowl and added two teaspoons of cumin. Muffled voices came through the receiver. It sounded like Jo and Mom were discussing something. Kaley stirred the mixture until the cumin was evenly distributed through the salt. In the distance, she could hear an engine.

Kirsten came back on the line. "Are you ready? We'll be in the driveway in a few seconds."

"I hear you guys." Kaley grabbed her phone and the bowl of spice and salt and headed the few steps to the front door.

As she opened the door, tires screeched, and Dad's pickup whipped into Tina's driveway. Right behind her family was the familiar glowing pale blue figure. However, it didn't need asphalt. It was cutting across the field and heading straight for the truck.

She stepped onto the tiny porch, scooped a handful of her mixture from the bowl, and tossed it in the air. With a bit of concentration, she gathered the grains so they whirled above her head.

Mom, Jo, and Kirsten baled out of the white truck and ran for the steps.

With a thrust of her hand, Kaley aimed the cumin and salt at the specter where it floated above the lawn. It shrieked when the grains swirled around and through it. At the same time, Mila screamed from further in the trailer.

Mom and Jo grabbed Kaley's arms and dragged her inside. Their actions broke her concentration. The salt and cumin landed on the wet grass. Kaley tried to collect her ammunition, but the salt dissolved, and the cumin soaked up the leftover rain and became too heavy to pick up with air alone.

It didn't matter. The specter shrieked in pain again and faded from sight.

Mila raced down the short hallway in her pink and blue pajamas and threw her arms around Kaley's waist. "Why does that thing keep coming here?" she asked between sobs.

Thankfully, Kirsten grabbed the bowl from Kaley and closed the front door so Kaley could comfort the little girl.

"It's nothing, sweetie," Kaley said. She knelt to hug Mila and stroke her hair.

"What's all the shouting about?" Noah said sleepily.

Kaley looked over Mila's shoulder. The boy stood at the edge of the hallway, blearily rubbing his eyes. His hair stood at weird angles.

"The ghost came back," Mila sobbed.

Jo knelt beside Kaley. "Sweetie, have you seen this thing before?"

Mila nodded and sniffed. "Mommy says it's my imagination."

Noah groaned. "Mila, you're the only one that's seen your ghost."

"No, she isn't," Kaley said gently though the kid was irritating her. "We've all seen it." She motioned to indicate her family standing around her.

Noah blinked. "You have?"

Before Kaley could answer, the front door swung open. Tina stepped inside, a confused look on her face. She reeked of cigarette smoke and alcohol. "What the devil is going on here?"

Kaley held her breath as she closed Mila's bedroom door behind her, but the little girl didn't so much as stir. Noah had been easy to get back to bed. He had merely rolled his eyes in preteen disgust at the drama before he retreated to his bedroom and slammed the door.

However, Mila wouldn't even let Tina touch her.

"You didn't believe me," the little girl sobbed. "Everyone here saw the ghost, but you said I lied."

At Tina's stricken expression, Mom pulled her aside while Kaley comforted Mila. Once in her bedroom, Kaley explained she'd cast a protective spell, and there was no way the ghost could get in the doublewide. Mila insisted Kaley needed to start teaching her magick, and she wouldn't lay down until Kaley pinky-swore. She hoped she hadn't just lied to the little girl.

Kaley sang old lullabies until Mila drifted back to sleep. Kaley walked carefully down the short hall, trying not to make much noise and wake the kids again. When she entered the living room, everyone turned to stare at her.

Tina huddled in the brown plaid armchair that matched her couch. Black mascara stains streaked down her cheeks. "I never saw it."

"Neither did Miz Rose," Kaley answered. She sat next to Mom who wrapped her right arm around Kaley's shoulders.

"You did some quick thinking tonight, sweetie." Mom squeezed her tight. "I'm proud of you. Both of you." She wrapped her left arm around Kirsten.

"Why is this thing at my place if it was haunting Rose?" Tina asked. "Is it after my little girl?"

"We don't know." Jo perched on Tina's brown ottoman that didn't quite match the colors of the couch and chair. She shook her head. "This thing isn't acting like a normal specter. It should be focusing on one person or one place." She looked at Kaley. "Did you get any more out of Mila?"

Kaley shook her head. "I didn't try to either. She was pretty upset."

"Should I keep her home from school tomorrow?" Tina examined each of their faces, searching for reassurance.

"The only Normal this thing has gone near is Rose—" Mom started.

"That we know of," Jo bit out.

"What if I meet Mila and Noah here when the bus drops them off?" Kirsten said. "A text already went out earlier today that the girl's basketball conditioning is cancelled for tomorrow. Coach Park's mom had a heart attack over the weekend."

Mom frowned. "I don't like that idea. Jo, Tina, and I will all still be at work."

"And Kaley will be a cheerleader practice." Kirsten shrugged off Mom's arm and leaned forward. "Between Kaley's spell and

Tina's wards, the specter couldn't get inside tonight. I can add another layer of protection tomorrow."

"Trying to steal my job, sis," Kaley teased.

"This isn't babysitting." Kirsten's big brown eyes were super serious. "This is us watching out for each other. We're the only witches who live in this town, and this thing seems to be attracted to us."

"What about Miz Rose?" Kaley said.

"She's been my friend for nearly thirty years." Jo exhaled forcefully, sending her loose strands of hair dancing. "It's possible she's carrying some of my energy just by the length of our proximity. I can put out some feelers at the coffee shop tomorrow. Very carefully. See if anyone else has seen this thing. And if it shows up at Rose's house again, she can come stay with me."

"Sounds like we have a plan," Mom said as she rose. "Let's get out of here so Tina can get some sleep."

Kaley swallowed her own fear while she stood, too. Mom's arm around her had been so comforting. But if she was going to push Mom and Dad for more autonomy, then she needed to suck it up an act like an adult.

Just like she had for Mila.

Everyone said their goodnights. Jo insisted she was riding with Kaley in Mom's car.

"I'm sorry I put you and your sister at risk," Jo murmured as Kaley followed the pickup back into town.

"It's not your fault," Kaley replied. "This whole thing is freaky as all get out. I get the specter having a grudge against me after our tussle this afternoon, but why was it hanging around Tina's place for the last few weeks? Or even Miz Rose's house?"

"I don't know, sweetie," Jo said.

The worried sound in her great-aunt's voice bothered Kaley more than she wanted to admit. While she grew up, if Mom didn't know the answer to something supernatural, Jo did. But for neither of them to know what the heck this blue entity was?

Kaley resisted the urge to shake her head as she drove down the county road. For the first time, she questioned the safety of the little village she called home. And she didn't like that feeling.

Not one darn bit.

Chapter 7

Kirsten stumbled into first period on Tuesday morning, clutching her large triple mocha as if her life depended on it. Maybe it did. Thank Goddess, Mrs. Tharp allowed drinks in her class. Sips from the steaming take-out cup from Jo's coffee shop were the only thing keeping Kirsten's eyes open this morning.

After spending half the night paging through both Mom and Grandma Charlie's Books of Shadows, Kirsten was rather peeved she hadn't found anything regarding the unusual entity she and Kaley encountered yesterday.

The dang thing looked like a specter and acted like a poltergeist. Also, it didn't seem to be attached to a particular person, place, or thing. She'd assumed it had followed Kaley out to the Eisler family's trailer, but if Mila had seen it before, that couldn't be the case. And how did Miz Rose fit in to all of this?

Donny Fryer slung his wiry body into the seat next to Kirsten. "Hey, is everything all right with Kaley?"

Oh, Goddess! She couldn't deal with the werecoyote this morning.

"She's fine." Kirsten slurped her mocha as she pulled out her American Literature homework.

"Yeah, but it's not like her to not text me back," Donny said. "I saw something in the woods near the Killbuck River—"

"No one wants hear about you running naked through the

woods, Fryer," Amelia Ryder snapped and flipped back her perfectly coiffed blue curls, the hue matching the West Holmes Knights' colors. She went to a specialist in Columbus for touch-ups every two weeks during football season. "Now get out of my seat."

Donny snorted as he glared at Amelia. "Never mind, Kirsten. It was probably some poor animal caught in the head cheerleader's toxic waste dump created by the crap she dyes her hair with."

"Was it blue—" Kirsten started to ask.

The second bell rang.

"Mr. Fryer, please take your assigned desk." Mrs. Tharp glared at him over the tops of her black cat's-eye glasses. Even though she was in her mid-thirties like Tina, she leaned toward a '50s style, including Peter Pan collars, flared skirts, and sensible shoes.

Donny stood, but Kirsten silently said, *We'll talk after class*.

He nodded and sauntered over to his seat closer to the front.

"I don't know what your sister sees in him," Amelia muttered under her breath as she sat down.

"She doesn't think she's better than everyone else like some people on the squad," Kirsten said mildly.

Amelia settled for glaring at her. Kirsten had to agree with Jo. If it weren't for the Rainier Outing, Amelia would have gotten some of her cronies to do some mean girl shit to both Kirsten and Kaley.

Kirsten barely paid attention to Mrs. Tharp's litany of announcements. Their specter had messed with hers and Kaley's phone reception at Miz Rose's yesterday afternoon. It only stood to reason the specter had done so again while Kaley was at the Eislers' last night.

Except Kirsten had been able to call Kaley while the specter chased the pickup truck. Had the specter wanted her and Kaley in the same spot, so it let her call go through?

She had too many questions and absolutely no answers. The end of first period couldn't come soon enough.

For once, Kirsten was happy she and Donny had their first two class periods together, and their second one was study hall.

"I thought you wanted to talk," he complained as they dodged other students in the hallway.

"In the library so we have some privacy," she said.

When they reached the study hall, Kirsten asked Mr. Price for a library pass. He didn't hand it over like he normally did. Instead, he eyed Donny suspiciously.

"I'm tutoring him in American Lit, and we can't talk in here." Kirsten pointed out.

The crinkles around Mr. Price's eyes eased and he nodded before he gave her the passes.

"Thank you, sir." She smiled and headed straight for the library, Donny on her heels.

It was a trick neither Kaley nor Donny had ever caught onto all their years in the public school system. Don't cause trouble, and the teachers didn't suspect you when you were really up to something. And Kirsten had tutored enough students Mr. Price didn't question her further.

Kirsten nodded to Ms. Kendall, the school librarian, and stalked toward the back table she normally used. The couple of nearby bookshelves blocked anyone from noticing her cast a circle so she could talk to Donny privately.

She slung her backpack on the table and sat. "What did you see in the woods last night?"

"First of all, why do you care all of the sudden?" He rested his heavily-used army surplus knapsack on the carpet and straddled the chair across the table from her.

"Because if it's the same thing we encountered yesterday, it wasn't letting your texts go through to Kaley."

Donny straightened. "This thing's after her?"

"We don't know for sure what's going on." Kirsten shrugged. "Please tell me what you saw, and I'll tell you what I know."

He rubbed the stubble on his chin. One thing in his favor as far as weird boy behavior went, he'd scored points as one of the first guys to get a decent beard. Being a werecoyote helped with that.

"It was about yay-big." He held up his hand to indicate the entity's height, around four feet. "It didn't have a specific shape like the ghosts at the Victorian House Museum. Kind of blobby. It glowed pale blue, and it stunk of ozone."

"Ozone?" She frowned at him and made a mental note of asking Kaley if she'd smelled anything at Miz Rose's yesterday when they were dealing with the alleged specter.

"Yeah." He gave her a rueful grin. "At first, I thought it was you or Kaley messing with me. It kept going back to Tina Eisler's trailer and circling her property like it was looking for a way in. I saw your mom's car in the driveway. That's why I tried texting her."

Kirsten propped her chin on her fists. "That's how Kaley described the entity, too."

Donny cocked his dark eyebrow. "Now, will you tell me what in Mother Wolf's teat is going on?"

She related the events at Miz Rose's house yesterday afternoon and Tina's house trailer last night. When she explained the problems with hers and Kaley's phones, Donny nodded.

"No reception sounds about right with the amount of magick that thing was throwing off."

"It didn't come after you?" she asked.

He shook his head. "I don't think it saw me. I stayed in the underbrush and behind trees as I followed it around."

"What time was this?"

"After midnight." He tilted his head. "Why?"

So the darn thing just wandered around the woods by the river after it had chased them in Dad's pickup last night?

Kirsten didn't realize she'd spoken aloud until Donny replied, "It seems so. I followed it out of curiosity, but it wasn't causing any harm as far as I knew." Again, he shrugged. "If I'd known it was harassing you guys and Miz Rose, I would've kept a closer eye on it."

She smiled at him. "Thanks for the tip about the ozone. That changes things a little bit."

"How so?" He seemed genuinely curious. This was probably the longest conversation the two of them ever had.

"Another witch could have raised the specter."

"No shit." He whistled softly. "You guys can do that?"

"It comes under the heading of an incredibly stupid idea, but yeah, we can." She grimaced. Could Noah or Mila have accidentally brought someone back from the afterlife? She certainly hadn't done it, and she didn't think Kaley would have done something that irresponsible.

An adult? Definitely not the ones she personally knew, which brought her back to an unknown witch in the county.

"So, there's possibly another witch in Millersburg we don't

know about?" Donny repeated Mom's suspicion from last night and Kirsten's own thoughts.

"Could be, but why—"

Donny snorted derisively. "Why was my daddy crazy enough to get involved with the Unseelie? We may have extra abilities Normals don't, but that doesn't make us any less human. And therefore, any less stupid."

Maybe she hadn't given Donny enough credit. Ever.

"Thanks for telling me what you saw." She smiled at him. "And for listening to me work this out."

Before he could say anything, something buzzed. He pulled out his phone and examined the screen.

"And that is your sister finally texting me back." He thumbs darted across the screen as he typed a reply.

Kirsten shook her head, leaned back in her chair, and pulled a novel from her backpack. "She's going to lose her phone again if Mrs. Freshwater catches her texting in World History."

Another buzz, and he started laughing. "She's pissed we didn't wait until she could join us."

"Then you guys need to sit with me at lunch instead of at the jocks and cheerleaders' tables," Kirsten shot back.

"Will do, boss." Donny shoved his phone back in his pocket, grabbed his backpack and pulled out a notebook. "If you'll excuse me, I do need to get my Spanish homework done during study hall."

She waved a hand to indicate he should do so and opened her novel. But no matter how she tried, she couldn't focus on N.K. Jemisin's latest book. If that specter was stalking her twin, it could be in the school right now. Considering how close that thing came to killing them both yesterday, the odds were someone at West Holmes could get seriously hurt if it came to the school.

And Kirsten didn't know how she'd handle it if that happened because she had no clue of how to get rid of the quasi-specter or whatever the heck it was.

Chapter 8

After school in the gym locker, Kaley changed into leggings, shorts, turtleneck, and t-shirt. Even though the day had been bright and sunny, it was still cold thanks to the front that brought in yesterday's rain. The coach insisted on practicing outside this afternoon, and it got dark early this time of year.

Kaley was pulling on her hoodie when someone shoved her from behind. She stumbled forward but caught herself. A short yank got the neckline past her head as she whirled around.

Amelia Ryder stood behind her, and her buddies Jennifer Rudlow and Madison Kenney flanked each side of Amelia. The other three cheerleaders watched with frowns on their faces as they also changed for practice.

"What the hell, Amelia?" Kaley snapped.

"You got a problem with me, Wilson?" The head cheerleader had an ugly expression and clenched fists.

"What are you talking about?" Kaley had learned to be wary of Amelia since kindergarten. Her moods changed faster than Ohio weather.

"Your sister says you think you're better than me." Amelia followed with a sneer that made her look even uglier for such a pretty girl. She tossed her blue-dyed curls.

Kaley sighed and rolled her eyes. "And if I text Kirsten, what is she going to say really happened?"

"She'll lie. All witches do."

Jennifer and Madison nodded at Amelia's awful words.

"In fact," she continued. "You probably hexed the coach to make the squad every year."

"Well, at least I'd be using my natural talents." Kaley smiled sweetly. "Instead of having my daddy pay my way to my position." It was no secret Mr. Ryder had donated a ton of money to the campaigns of several of the school board members. They in turn pressured the principal, who in turned threatened to fire Ms. Cross as the varsity cheerleading coach if Amelia wasn't made head cheerleader for her senior year.

The other three girls tittered at the insult. Jennifer and Madison looked to their leader for their cues. Amelia's pale complexion turned bright red. Kaley saw the slap coming a mile away and ducked. Amelia's momentum pulled her off balance. She stumbled, and her knee hit the painted concrete floor with a sickening crack.

She screamed and collapsed onto the floor, cradling her injured joint.

"What is going on in here?" Ms. Cross rushed into the girl's locker room followed by a couple of the assistant football coaches.

Jennifer pointed at Kaley. "Kaley did it! She's pissed that Amelia got the head cheerleading position and attacked her!"

"I didn't touch her!" Kaley yelled back.

The locker room erupted as the other three cheerleaders backed up Kaley, and Madison backed Jennifer's version of events. Meanwhile, Amelia's wailing grew exponentially as one of the assistant football coaches tried to examine her knee.

"The rest of you out on the field." Ms. Cross jabbed an index finger in the direction of the door. "Now!"

Jennifer and the rest of the girls scurried to obey. But when Kaley tried to follow them, Ms. Cross held up a palm.

"Not you, Wilson. You're going to the principal's office."

"But, I didn't—"

"Are you injured?" Ms. Cross said with a scowl on her face.

Kaley's heart sank. Ms. Cross was more worried about her job than she was about being just.

"No, ma'am," Kaley ground out.

"Then go to the principal's office." Ms. Cross turned her back and focused on the sobbing Amelia.

Kaley clinched her own fists. Dammit, this wasn't her fault! Mr. Denton, the other assistant football coach, gave her a sympathetic look and inclined his head in the direction of the door.

There was nothing more she could accomplish here. She retrieved her belongings and stalked toward the high school's administrative offices.

Kaley was sitting in Principal Reed's office when the paramedics loaded Amelia into the ambulance. Seconds later, its siren wailed and its lights flashed as it sped off toward Pomerene Hospital.

"Are you listening to me, Miss Wilson?" Principal Reed said rather loudly.

She turned back to him. "You said that this is a no tolerance school. However, I didn't raise a hand to Amelia Ryder."

"Did you use magick?" Principal Reed said.

Kaley blinked. He couldn't be serious.

"If I wanted to hurt her, I wouldn't have ducked her slap," Kaley spat. "And I would have used my fists."

The principal shook his index finger at her. "You just watch that attitude, young lady. I can expel you for threatening another student."

Kaley inhaled and slowly exhaled to calm herself down. "I didn't threaten anyone. You asked me a question. Was that question rhetorical or were you serious?"

"Did you use magick?" he repeated. "Yes or no?"

"No."

"Fine." He leaned back in his chair. "You're suspended for three days for fighting in school. Now I suggest you go home and think about what you've done. I'll be calling your parents."

"I can't go home just yet," she said.

"You're seventeen." He rose abruptly and reached for the phone. "I can have you arrested for trespassing."

"And what will Sheriff Birkheimer say if something happens to me while I walk home? There's no sidewalks between here and downtown Millersburg." She met Principal Reed's gaze squarely. "Donny Fryer was supposed to give me a ride home today because my sister has our mom's car, and she's already left because she's watching a friend's kids after school. So if you want me off school property, you need to call my dad."

Principal Reed released the phone receiver and slowly sat back down. "Go wait in the football stands for Mr. Fryer. I'd better not catch you any place else."

"Yes, sir." Kaley stood and hurried from his office. The lump in her throat threatened to turn into full-blown tears, but the last thing she'd do was give Principal Reed, or more especially Amelia and her cronies, the satisfaction of knowing they'd gotten to her.

When Kaley reached the stadium stands, Ms. Cross stared at her from across the field. But when Kaley didn't join them, Ms. Cross returned her attention to the remaining squad members.

Kaley climbed to the fourth row so she could keep an eye out for Donny. She pulled out her phone and took a steadying breath before she hit the speed dial for Mom's office.

Her phone rang once before Mom picked up. "Kaley, what's wrong?"

"Mom, you're about to get a call from Principal Reed." Kaley's mouth went dry, and it took a couple of tries before her story spilled.

On the other end of the line, Mom sighed. "Thank you for telling me, sweetie. Let me talk to your dad." She paused a moment before she said, "Reed is on the other line. We'll discuss this more over dinner. Do you need a ride, or is Donny still driving you home?"

"Yeah, he is."

"I'll see you later, sweetie. We love you." The line clicked.

Kaley swallowed hard to keep the tears at bay. She pulled out her English Lit book and started reading tomorrow's assignment.

She knew it wasn't right, but part of her really wanted to hex Amelia and her cronies. Nothing really harmful, just something embarrassing. Like a terrible case of acne, or making their hair fall out.

But if she did, she'd be the nasty witch everyone was accusing her of being. Despite what Aunt Jo thought, the Rainier Outing wasn't a good thing for everybody. Maybe this was why Kirsten was so adamant about leaving Millersburg.

Chapter 9

Kirsten stood at the end of the driveway when the huge, yellow bus with "West Holmes School District" stenciled on the side braked in front of the Eisler's trailer. Mila waved to their driver before she bounded down the steps. Noah wore the sullen expression he'd adopted over the summer as he followed his sister off the bus.

When he was clear, the bus driver closed the doors. The red blinking lights winked out, and in a wave of noxious diesel exhaust, the bus trundled down the county road to take home the rest of the elementary kids.

"Can we play Trouble or Monopoly or rummy or—" Mila said in a rush as the three of them walked up the asphalt drive.

"Whoa, slow down." Kirsten laughed. "You know the rules. We all need to get our homework done first."

"But we can have snacks, right?" Mila batted her big brown eyes.

"Your mom said celery and peanut butter and string cheese," Kirsten said. Kaley had gone through the list of do's and don't's, but Tina had left a voice-mail with the same restrictions and permissions.

In case Kaley had left something out.

"Dad would let us have chips," Noah grumbled.

Kirsten wasn't sure how to respond to the boy's comment.

Tina and Ken divorced over a year ago. Despite their personal issues, they'd always seemed to do right by Noah and Mila.

"Dad bribes us," Mila spat back. "If he really loved us, he wouldn't have left."

"Mom drove him out," Noah said with the confident authority of a preteen. "You're too young to know what was really going on."

"Mom did not—" Mila cried.

"Okay, okay. That's enough." Kirsten held up her hands. "Your parents' problems are not your problems. And they both love you."

They climbed the steps to the tiny porch and entered the trailer before Mila said in a small voice, "Mom said we may have to stay with Dad if the ghost comes back."

"It's not a ghost," Noah said angrily. "It's a specter. Get it right. And what's wrong with staying at Dad's?"

"Skylar's mean!" Mila stomped her foot.

Kirsten swallowed her own opinion of Ken's girlfriend. Skylar was only two years older than Kirsten. Not to mention an absolute twit. Her parents had hired Kirsten to tutor her, but Kirsten quit when Skylar tried to blackmail her into taking Skylar's final exams for the twit.

If Ken was trying to force Skylar and the kids to like each other, it was only going to blow up in his face. But Kirsten couldn't blame Tina for wanting to protect her children.

"You were mean to her first!" Noah shouted back.

Kirsten added a touch of magic to her voice to drown out the kids' arguing. "That's enough!"

They both looked up at her, their eyes wide.

"No one's going anywhere anytime soon." She pulled her jacket off and hung it on a peg on the wall-mounted coat rack.

"Get your coats off and grab your homework. The sooner we get done, the sooner we can play a game."

Noah opened his mouth like he was about to argue, but Kirsten narrowed her eyes and inclined her head toward Mila, who was retrieving her materials from her backpack, silently daring him to say anything. His shoulders sagged in acquiescence.

"Fine," he mumbled. "But can we play video games instead?"

"We can do both as long as we get that homework done first."

That seemed to mollify Noah. While he hung up his coat and retrieved his own work, Kirsten got busy fixing their snacks.

Darkness had fallen and the three of them were in the middle of a space battle on the kids' gaming system. This meant poor Agatha could safely sleep on Tina's bed unmolested. Kirsten had initially worried about Mila playing out of her depth, but she'd won the last three rounds and was about to cream both Kirsten and Noah for a fourth when headlights flashed through the sheer living room curtains.

"Mom's home early!" Mila dropped her controller, leapt to her feet, and raced for the front door.

"Don't open it!"

Mila stopped at Kirsten's sharp command. The girl turned to Kirsten with an alarmed expression.

Kirsten set her controller on the coffee table and climbed to her feet. "Always check to see who's out there first."

Mila leaned over and peeked around the edge of the closest curtain. She turned back to Kirsten with an alarmed expression. "I don't know who that is."

Noah leaned back in the armchair and pulled aside the left curtain panel. "It's Kaley with some guy." He turned to Kirsten. "Who's the were?"

While some tension eased with Noah's announcement, the rest drained away when Kirsten peeked outside over Mila's head. "That's our friend Donny. It was easier for him to drop her off here instead of doubling back into town."

"I can't wait until I'm in high school," Noah muttered as he dropped his end of the curtains.

"What's wrong with grade school?" Mila asked with a cross expression.

"I'll be able to drive," Noah retorted.

A knock on the door interrupted the brewing sibling battle. Kirsten opened the door. "You're . . ." The words died in her throat as she took in her sister's anguished expression.

"I just got suspended."

Even Noah looked serious as Kaley spilled her story of what happened in the high school girls' locker room. Donny leaned against the wall between the kitchen and the living room, a scowl plastered on his face.

Agatha wandered into the living room. She sniffed Donny's jeans before she wound a figure-eight pattern around and between his legs, giving him permission to be in her family's home.

"But that's not fair if this Amelia started the fight," Noah stated.

Donny snorted. "No shit, kid." Agatha meowed in what sounded like agreement.

Kirsten glared at him as did Kaley.

"You said a bad word," Mila whispered in horror.

"I'm sorry." Donny smiled wickedly at the eight-year-old. "You act like the twins, and I forgot you're not our age." His answer seemed to mollify Mila.

"All right," she said. "As long as you don't use any more bad words."

Donny pulled off his letterman jacket and hung it up. "Why don't I take look around outside while I'm here?"

"Can I watch you change shape?" Mila jiggled with excitement on the floor.

"No," Kirsten said at the same time as Donny and Kaley. "Your mom would get pretty upset if you saw him naked because he's a lot older than you."

"He's only nine years older," Mila drawled. "It's not that much."

"I don't feel comfortable about it," Donny said. "So it ain't gonna happen."

Agatha meowed again and took a couple of steps toward the hall.

"No, you're not watching either." He turned to Noah. "Wanna show me to your bathroom and stand guard?"

Noah snickered. "Sure." He slung his legs off the arm of the chair, stood, and beckoned Donny to follow him.

Agatha rumbled low in her chest, not quite a purr but not quite a growl either. Kirsten didn't want to speculate about what the cat was thinking. Agatha jumped up on the back of the couch and flicked her tail in Kirsten's face.

Once the boys were out of sight, Mila got up and flopped next to Kaley on the couch. "He's cute." The little girl's eyes twinkled. "Is he your boyfriend?"

"Nope, we're just friends," Kaley said. "Besides he likes someone else."

"Who?" Kirsten looked at her sister. This was the first she'd heard of Donny being interested in anything besides football and hunting.

"Not my secret to tell," Kaley answered mildly. "Unfortunately, the girl in question won't give him the time of day."

Kirsten groaned. "Please tell me it's not one of the other cheerleaders."

Anxiety flitted across Kaley's features and flared against Kirsten's mental shields.

"Ouch, I'm sorry." Kirsten grimaced. "Have you called Mom or Dad?"

"Yeah, I called Mom." Kirsten's eyes watered. "She was fit to be tied, of course, but I gave her the heads-up before Reed called her. She insisted she be the one to tell Dad."

They both tried to ignore the sounds of bones and flesh rearranging along with the grunts that came from the Eisler's bathroom. However, Mila kept trying to peer down the hall. So did Agatha.

Mila looked over at Kirsten. "Doesn't changing his shape hurt him?"

"It can be . . . uncomfortable," Kirsten said. "It's why most weres prefer privacy when they shift."

Nails scratched against the flimsy bathroom door. A second later, Donny trotted out on four legs. Noah followed him into the living room, an expression of pure hero worship on his face.

Kirsten had to admit Donny was an attractive coyote. The majority of his coat was brown, shading to a reddish hue at his head, paws, and tail. He shook himself once before he headed for the front door. He pointedly looked over his shoulder at her and back at the round knob gracing the Eislers' front door.

"Oops." She grinned. "I'm used to you waltzing through our house." When Mom and Dad had done some remodeling a few years ago, Dad insisted on the lever-style door handles, claiming he was tired of Donny scratching up the house paint.

Maybe that was the real reason Donny hung around their house so much. Other than the football coaches, Dad was the one adult male who actually showed some interest in the guy, and not for what he could get out of poor Donny either.

Kirsten stood and crossed to the door. "Bark when you come back."

I'm not a dog. With a defiant flick of his bushy tail, he darted outside. But she knew he would do as she asked once he'd investigated the Eisler's quarter-acre lot and the surrounding cornfields and woods.

"That is so awesome," Noah exclaimed. "I wish I were a were instead of a witch."

"But then you'd have to worry about fleas," Kirsten said. Agatha meowed.

Kaley giggled, a good sound considering how upset she still was. "Oh, my Goddess! I forgot about the time Dad gave him a flea bath."

Kirsten and Kaley took turns of telling the stories of when Donny and they were Noah and Mila's age and the pranks they pulled and the antics they gotten into. Kirsten was secretly glad. It kept Kaley's mind off her own problems, and they kept the kids from thinking about the real reason Donny sniffed around outside. Mila was easy to distract, but Noah was no fool.

Roughly twenty minutes later, a sharp bark came from the

tiny porch. Kirsten jumped up and let Donny back into the trailer. He trotted straight for the bathroom, his tail high which, meant he found something.

A couple of minutes later, he strolled into the living room, still tugging on his heavy metal band t-shirt. His feet were bare. He flopped into the armchair and said nothing.

"And?" Kirsten prompted. If he loved dramatics so much, why didn't he try out for the school play?

He grinned at her impatience. "Nothing but the Eislers' and your scents out in the yard, but there's a sh—" He stopped himself and glanced at Mila. "Sorry, there's a ton of ozone in the cornfield next door and in the woods across the road." He waved in the direction where Kaley said she originally saw the specter last night.

"I backtracked it down to the river bank where I saw the specter last night, but I couldn't pick anything else. Sorry." He shrugged. "Dang, I'm starving. You guys have anything to eat around here?"

"We have celery and peanut butter," Mila offered enthusiastically.

Despite needing meat, he was gracious to the little girl. "That would be great. Thanks."

She rushed over to their tiny kitchen table and retrieved the plate of celery sticks that only Kirsten had touched. Mila and Noah had plowed through the string cheese.

Mila hovered over Donny as he took the first bite. Despite the normal blur of a were's thoughts, their emotions were rather vivid. Despite Donny's hatred of anything green, his smile didn't waver as he chewed the first bite.

"Thanks. That really hits the spot, Mila."

She practically danced back to the couch at the older boy's approval.

The front door opened, and a very tired looking Tina walked in. She frowned at Donny and then at Kirsten. "I thought my rules were clear. No boys while you're babysitting my kids."

"He's not a boy, Mom," Mila protested. "He's a werewolf."

"Werecoyote," Donny automatically corrected.

"I can see that, sweetie," Tina said. "It doesn't explain why he's in my living room."

"You've met Donny at our house." Kaley jumped up. "I didn't think it would be a big deal when I asked him to drop me off here after school—"

"You don't have to cover for me, sis," Kirsten said. She stood, too. "I'm sorry, Tina. I asked Donny to drop by after football practice and take a sniff around your property. Since we grew up with him, we think of him more as a brother. I didn't mean to break your rules."

An amused glint flashed in Tina's dark eyes. "You're forgiven this once. So, what did you find, Donny?" Agatha slunk along the back of the couch and head-butted Tina's arm, demanding attention.

He shrugged. "From the amount of ozone, I think another witch is messing with you guys."

Agatha meowed again as if saying, "Told you so."

Chapter 10

Kaley sat at the dinner table and poked at her meatloaf. As much as she'd rather talk about Donny's theory regarding the specter, Mom insisted on discussing what happened at the high school and Kaley's suspension first.

Dad wiped his hands down his face and leaned his chin on his clasped hands before he looked at her again. Dark circles marred the pale skin beneath his eyes. She hated his sad expression. And she hated even more that she was the cause of it.

"I guess our years of peace and quiet are gone," he said. "We need to be ready for the torches and pitchforks."

"Ethan!" Mom stared at him aghast. "How could you say that to our daughters?"

Dad cocked his head. "Really? You can't tell me you and the rest of your coven haven't been expecting something like this for the last eleven years, Rachel. I'm not happy about our girls being the first ones the Normals decided to make examples of, but there it is!" He banged the back of his hand on the dining room table, making the silverware jump.

"So what do we do?" Kirsten said. "Amelia lied about what I said. She lied about what Kaley did. We've got to do something—"

Despite the distance between them over the last couple of years, a warm feeling spread through Kaley at her twin's defense.

"Don't even think about any 'accidents,' you two." Dad's

right index finger pointed at each of them in turn. "If something unusual happens to Amelia now, you will be the first ones everybody in town will blame."

Kaley threw down her fork, and it clattered against the ceramic plate. "You think we don't know that!"

"Our girls wouldn't do something like that," Mom protested.

"No, Dad's right." Kirsten leaned her elbows on the table. "That's why I wanted to talk about what Donny found out over at the Eislers' place first. If it is an outside witch messing with us, Amelia's in danger. She'd be the easiest way to discredit us."

"Why would any witch care?" Kaley looked at her twin. "You don't even want to be here. You keep going on about how boring Millersburg is."

Now, Dad and Mom stared at Kirsten, too.

"Is this true, honey?" Mom asked.

Kirsten's mouth twisted. "Which part? That Donny only detected ozone outside of Tina's parcel, or that I don't like living here?"

"The second," Dad said. "Is this why you've been pushing to go out of state for college?"

Kirsten stared at her plate. "Yeah."

Mom and Dad exchanged looks, and Kaley couldn't block their emotions battering her psyche. Not the soul-searing hurt she felt. Theirs was more like disappointment.

"I think we need to focus on the Amelia situation first," Dad said. He leaned back and ran his hands through his short, dark hair. "Especially if it is connected to this specter roaming around the area. Did it show up at Tina's tonight while you girls were there?"

Both Kaley and Kirsten shook their heads.

"We should give Jimmy a call and give him a heads-up," Dad

said, looking at Mom. "Both he and Julia are up on this supernatural stuff." Not only had Dad gone to high school with Sheriff Jimmy Birkheimer, they'd been best friends since kindergarten and on the basketball team together during West Holmes High boys' last run for the state championship. They still fished together at Crazy Matt Jessup's pond once a week during the summer. Plus, Jimmy had participated in the Battle of Millersburg with Mom and Aunt Jo. He'd been the twins' Uncle Jimmy all their lives.

Mom's lips pursed before she nodded. "I don't like it, but it might not be a bad idea. At least, Julia Wolford is technically Family." Mom said the last word with an emphasis on the capital "F". Family were Normals related by blood or marriage to a supernatural. And Julia's stepmom was the pack leader of the Killbuck werecoyotes who'd split and moved to Las Vegas. The remaining Killbuck pack members learned the hard way not to mess with Deputy Julia Wolford when she moved back to Holmes County. She'd been trained to fight by vampire enforcers.

"If it is another witch, someone's going to need to put protections in place for Amelia and her family," Kaley said. She didn't like Amelia, but neither did she want to see her get hurt. At least, not any more than she already was. "They're not going to let me anywhere near them."

"Tina working at the hospital will be in our favor then." Mom smiled. "I'll call her after dinner."

"And I'll call Jimmy," Dad said.

"In the meantime, we need a contingency plan," Kirsten said. "We can hide out in the Levys' root cellar temporarily—"

"That's not funny," Kaley snapped.

"I'm not joking," Kirsten said quietly. "Mary's been worried about something like this happening for a few years now.

It wouldn't be the first time they or the Millers have sheltered supernaturals. They're Family, too." Mary's brother Joshua had taken over their great-grandfather Thomas's farm after the elderly Amish man had been killed by the wanagamesak. Thomas's sister Anne stayed in the root cellar on the farm when she came for visits before she and her husband took the cure for vampirism.

"I don't think anyone has to go into hiding just yet," Mom said. She turned to Dad. "Or pull out the armor and fire extinguishers. I'm going in to talk to the principal in the morning. We'll get this suspension straightened out."

"How, Mom?" Kaley waved her right hand. "The other three girls stood up for me, and no one listened."

"There's ways," Mom said primly. At Dad's skeptical look, she stated, "Not all of it has to do with magick, Ethan."

"I'm afraid to ask what dirt you have on Lester Reed," Dad said with mock dismay.

"You'd be surprised what goes on in this town." Mom winked at him.

"I doubt it. I'm a veterinarian," Dad said dryly. "And this is Ohio, where the men are men and the sheep are scared."

"Da-a-ad!" Kaley wailed. "Not at the dinner table. That's gross!"

"Not as gross as what they had to do to produce us," Kirsten said.

"Maybe I'm the one who needs to move away," Kaley grumbled. She snatched up her fork, speared a chunk of roasted potato, and popped it in her mouth. Maybe the rest of the family would follow suit, and they'd shut up while they chewed.

After dinner, the girls cleaned up the dining room and kitchen. As Kaley scrubbed the CorningWare dish Mom baked the meatloaf in with a plastic sponge, she sighed.

"We're never going to get a dishwasher," Kirsten said as she dried the last plate.

"That's not my problem." Kaley rinsed the dish and set it in the drainer.

"You're that worried Mom will get you back in school tomorrow?" Kirsten quipped. She started toweling off the silverware.

"I'm actually a little worried about Amelia," Kaley admitted.

Kirsten tossed the utensils into their respective tray slots and slammed the drawer with excessive force before she propped her fists on her hips. "You've got to be kidding me. You two have never been real friends. Not to mention, she took something I said and twisted it around in order to pick a fight with you."

"You didn't hear the sound when her knee hit the floor." Kaley released the stopper and waited for the water to drain.

"Well, she shouldn't have tried to hit you, should she?" Kirsten said.

Penn came in and rubbed against Kaley's legs before he jumped on the counter. He pawed at the Tupperware container with the remainder of the meatloaf.

"One attempted slap doesn't equate to a smashed kneecap," she said.

Penn batted the plastic box more forcefully.

"All right. All right." Kaley grabbed the container before Penn swatted it off the counter. "You can have one bite, but that's it. The rest is for Mom and Dad's lunches tomorrow." She lifted a corner of the lid, and pinched off a tiny bite. He daintily took the morsel and looked up at her, pleading for more.

Teller raced across the linoleum, leapt onto the counter beside Penn, and pushed his brother aside, all while meowing quite loudly.

"Sound asleep until you hear someone else getting food, huh?" Kaley muttered. She gave Teller a bite, too, before she snapped the lid back on the box and placed it in the refrigerator.

"So, we're going to avoid the real problems?" Kirsten reached for the baking dish and started drying it.

Kaley faced her sister. "What if you and Donny are right? What if another witch is conjuring this specter or controlling it in an effort to drive us out of town?"

Kirsten frowned as she put away the CorningWare dish. "You made a good point earlier. Why would another witch even bother with Millersburg? We're simply an offshoot of Brown Dog Coven. And no one has messed with Brown Dog in over two hundred years. Not since the founding of Cleveland."

"So it's personal." A shiver raced up Kaley spine and back down again.

Kirsten hung the dish towel on the handle of the stove and started ticking points off on her fingers. "Miz Rose was our 4-H advisor when we both started. You babysit Tina's kids quite a bit—"

"But why?" Kaley threw her hands up. "Who have we pissed off enough they would do something like this to a couple of high school kids?"

"Another high school kid," Kirsten said.

Kaley crossed her arms and cocked her head. "Oh, come on! Amelia Ryder isn't a witch."

Both Penn and Teller meowed their agreement.

"No, but she has money." Kirsten grimaced. "Or rather her

dad does. The Ryders wouldn't be the first Normals to hire an eclectic since the Outing."

"No." Kaley shook her head. "Not even Amelia is crazy enough to bust up her knee like that on purpose."

"Maybe she got mad because all of yesterday's stunts didn't scare you." Kirsten picked up Teller and stroked him under the chin.

"Then why has she been scaring poor little Mila for the last couple of weeks?" Kaley waved her right hand. "We didn't even know about the specter going to Tina's place until yesterday. Plus, there's no connection between Mila and Miz Rose."

"There's Noah," Kirsten stated firmly over Teller's loud purring. The gray tabby was positively limp in her arms. "He joined the 4-H club during Miz Rose's last year as advisor."

"Now you're really grasping at straws." Kaley held up both hands in surrender. "I'm going to bed." She headed for the living room.

Penn meowed piteously behind her.

She pivoted to face the gold tabby. "You're not a spoiled, helpless baby. You can walk." She whirled and stomped out of the kitchen.

But as Kaley climbed the steps to her room, she wondered if her sister were right. Amelia wanted to be top dog so bad. Maybe she did hire an eclectic. Maybe the swing and miss in the locker room was the Three-Fold Law coming back to bite the head cheerleader in the ass.

Kaley entered her room and flopped back first onto her mattress. A second later, Penn leapt up beside her and nudged her hand with his soft cheek.

"I'm sorry," she whispered. "I shouldn't have taken my bad

mood out on you." She stroked the gold tabby until he curled against her ribcage and purred.

Mom always said magick couldn't solve all problems.

So how the hell did she question Amelia about the specter or hiring an eclectic without causing more trouble?

Chapter 11

The loud pounding downstairs woke Kirsten. She grabbed her phone and checked the time. Ugh. Ten minutes before her alarm went off. So much for any extra sleep.

That's when she realized Teller wasn't curled up next to her like he usually was. He meowed loudly from the direction of her bedroom door. Male voices filtered up through the ancient heating grates from the floor below. Then Dad's voice rose.

"Dammit, Jimmy! Both girls have been here all night no matter what Ryder says!"

Kirsten jerked upright in her bed. Was Uncle Jimmy here in his professional capacity as sheriff?

She threw back her covers, hurried to the door, and opened it. Kaley's door across the hallway flew open at the same time.

"Did you—" Kirsten started to say.

"Yeah." Kaley scowled as the voices grew angrier.

Kirsten raced after her sister up the hall and down the staircase. The hardwood floorboards were cold, but she didn't want to waste time going back for her slippers. Penn and Teller whizzed past the girls and landed between Dad and Uncle Jimmy, hissing and spitting at the law officer. And Uncle Jimmy was definitely wearing his official uniform.

"What the devil?" The sheriff stared at the felines with their arched backs and their bared teeth as he stood in the entryway with Dad.

"Stop it, you two!" he snapped at the cats. "Or so help me, I will tranquilize both of you."

Dad didn't bluff, and Penn and Teller knew it. They lowered their fur and padded over to Kirsten and Kaley like nothing out of the ordinary had just happened.

Mom came out of the dining room. Like Dad, she was fully dressed.

"Didn't you have anyone watching Amelia Ryder last night?" she asked.

"Give me a little credit, Rachel." Jimmy scowled at Mom. "I had Deputy Wolford up there to keep an eye on things. And I deputized Tina Eisler as an emergency measure as soon as she arrived at the hospital this morning." He pushed his hat back and scratched his forehead.

The tension on Mom's face eased. "Would you like to join us for breakfast, Jimmy? We can discuss the reason for your visit over full stomachs."

"Thanks." He nodded to Mom. "I'm glad someone here has some sense." He glared at the cats as he said the last part. Penn and Teller turned their backs on him and sashayed past Mom, no doubt in search of the bacon Kirsten could smell.

"Girls, get dressed. I promise we won't talk until you get back down here. And you two in the kitchen better not touch my bacon!" Mom yelled over her shoulder.

A dejected meow filtered through the house.

"The specter showed up at the hospital?" Kirsten stared at Jimmy in disbelief. More over the layer of ketchup he poured over Mom's perfect light and fluffy scrambled eggs than his statement.

"Yep. Went straight to the Ryder girl's room just like you said, Rachel. About three a.m." He slurped his coffee with cream and sugar. "Thanks for not trying to feed me doughnuts." He winked at Mom.

"So why did you start off by asking where our daughters were last night, Jimmy?" Dad growled.

"Look, man, I gotta cover all the bases in an investigation whether I like it or not." The sheriff scooped a huge forkful of red-stained eggs into his mouth. Once he chewed and swallowed, he continued. "Ryder's making all kinds of noises about Kaley and Kirsten being out to hurt his daughter. Frankly, I already came by your place on my way to the hospital when I got the call this morning and checked the engines on all your cars. They were cold." He eyed Kaley, then Kirsten. "So, if one of you, or both, hitched a ride with a friend after your parents went to bed, you'd better tell me now."

"Nope." Kirsten shook her head. "We stayed in last night after we got home from watching Tina Eisler's kids. That was right before dinner. About six-thirty."

"How often have you used your parents' vehicles?" The sheriff pulled a notebook and a pen from his breast pocket.

"Dad's been dropping Mom off at the paper on his way to his clinic. We've been using Mom's car for school between cheerleading practice and basketball conditioning—" Kirsten started.

"Donny Fryer did give me a ride out to Tina Eisler's yesterday after football practice," Kaley interjected.

"Only because I drove out to the Eislers' in Mom's sedan after school. I was watching Tina's kids after school since the specter has been showing up at their place." Kirsten took a drink of her orange juice to give Jimmy the chance to scribble in his notebook. "And I asked Donny to come out to sniff around and catch the scent of who might be terrorizing poor Mila."

"Has Fryer seen the specter?" he asked.

"Yes, he saw it in the woods Monday night." She shrugged. "Since it didn't appear to be bothering anyone, he let it alone. Or he did until he asked me Tuesday morning why Kaley hadn't texted him back."

Jimmy grunted. "The spectral energy messed with your phones?"

"That's what we think." Kirsten nodded. "The two times it happened to us was when it's been around me or Kaley."

"Who else has seen this thing?" he asked.

"Well, Miz Rose didn't actually *see* the specter, but it has been tearing up her sunroom and kitchen," Kirsten said. "She came to Jo's coffee shop, asking for help Monday morning. Kaley and I chased it out of her house and laid down a protection spell to keep it from coming back inside."

"Rose Gleason?" Jimmy eyed her, his pen poised over his notepad.

"Well, duh!" Kaley looked at him like he'd grown an extra head.

He scowled at her. "Don't get lippy with someone who's changed your diaper, Kaley Josephine Wilson." He turned back to Kirsten. "Why didn't your Aunt Jo go over to Miz Rose's house? Those two have been tight for years."

Heat flooded Kirsten's face. She cleared her throat. "Because Miz Rose thought it was her brother haunting her. Neither Jo or I took it seriously after Rose had been imagining her mother haunting her for the last couple of years." She sucked in a deep breath. "I volunteered to check out the house after my shift to put Miz Rose's mind at ease since Jo couldn't go over until she closed up the coffee shop."

"Did you go over by yourself?" he asked, still scribbling in his notebook.

"No, sir." Goddess, the next part was going to look bad. "Mom sent Kaley to pick me up after my shift because of the rain so she tagged along over to Miz Rose's."

"And what happened at Rose's house?"

Kirsten laid out how the specter first used Rose's kitchen knives, then the broken glass and other objects in the Florida room to kill them. While she spoke, Kaley grabbed her varsity jacket to show Jimmy the slices from the glass and the matching cuts on her arms.

After they finished, he tapped his pen against his notepad for nearly a minute while his eggs grew cold.

"Are you going to tell my daughters not to leave town next?" Dad still looked peeved by this whole thing.

"Do I have to, Ethan?" the sheriff shot back.

Mom jumped in before the men started arguing again. "What happened at the hospital, Jimmy?"

"That's the odd part." The sheriff shook his head. "This specter of yours showed up on the same floor where Amelia Ryder is, like you suspected it would." He eyed Kaley. "Just to let you know, she's going in for reconstructive surgery this morning. She managed to screw up her knee pretty bad."

"Are you going to accuse me of deliberately hurting her, too?" Kaley's fury battered Kirsten's mental shields. The tablecloth fluttered against Kirsten's leg, and a breeze ruffled the napkins sitting in the Longaberger basket holder. Kaley was on the edge of losing control, and that wasn't going to help things.

Jimmy chuckled. "Hackles down, Kaley. You don't think I know the crap that goes on in this county? That's why I've been trying to talk your father into running for the school board."

"Then why—" Kirsten started to ask.

"Because I need my ducklings lined up when I talk to the county prosecutor." The sheriff shook his head. "I know your sister didn't do a damn thing to Amelia despite what she and her little posse of tramps are saying. Not everyone in town is on their side." He grinned. "Not to mention, karma's a bitch."

He turned back to Mom. "This time, your specter was visible to the Normals, too. Everyone I interviewed described a glowing, pale blue apparition."

"About the size of an early grade school child, right?" Kirsten wished he'd hurry with the details, but Uncle Jimmy liked spinning his stories.

"That's not what they saw." He pushed back his empty plate and leaned his elbows on the table. "Everyone, including Deputy Wolford, described the apparition as canine-shaped."

"What?" Kaley looked at him with an incredulous expression on her face.

A ripple of unease run through Kirsten. Unless the ghost or specter was originally a were, they just didn't change shapes like that. It was looking more and more like another witch was trying to get Kaley in trouble, and now they may be trying to point the finger at Donny, too. Like the guy needed any more grief. The universe had thrown him enough already.

She glanced at Mom, who had a troubled expression on her face, but her mental shields were closed tighter than Fort Knox.

"Did it hurt anyone?" Mom asked quietly.

"Naw," Jimmy drawled. "Deputy Wolford was prepared. The worst thing it did was scare Amelia and the nurses, one of whom dropped her tablet, and it broke. Well, everyone's cell phones weren't working for a bit, and the landlines were staticky as hell, but they weren't damaged. Everything but the dropped tablet worked just fine once Julia chased the specter away with the protection charm Jo supplied her."

Just like what the entity had done to their phones at Miz Rose's. Kirsten swallowed her bite of bacon. "But Mr. Ryder still wants you to arrest Kaley."

"On what grounds?" He smiled gently at her twin. "Scaring people isn't necessarily a crime."

He looked back at Mom. "I'm assuming since Jo's charm didn't blow up the hospital, this thing, whatever it is, isn't fae-related."

Mom shook her head. "Is everybody in the sheriff's department carrying their protective charms?"

He nodded. "A couple of the newbies were giving us older officers a rough time about it, but after Julia's new partner got a look at your apparition, he wet himself and decided I wasn't such a silly, superstitious old man after all."

"You're not old." Dad grinned, loosening up for the first time since the sheriff knocked on the door this morning. "You're my age."

"I hate to say this, but you're old, too." Jimmy pushed back his chair and stood. "Thanks for breakfast, Rachel. I appreciate it."

Mom and Dad rose as well and escorted him to the entryway.

"It's definitely not a specter if it's changing shape," Kirsten murmured.

"No shit, Sherlock," Kaley snapped. "The question is how do we find out who's behind this and catch 'em."

"It's something we can think about at school." Kirsten pushed back from the table and started clearing it. "Because it looks like you aren't going to enjoy any suspension."

"Crap. I have a physics quiz today." Kaley raced for the stairs.

When the thumping on the steps receded, Kirsten stalked over to the spice cupboard. Mom kept extra canisters of salt for protection and cleansing spells. Kirsten grabbed an unopened one and placed it in her backpack.

She wasn't precognitive, but something inside her said she might need the mineral before the end of the day.

Chapter 12

Later that same morning, Kaley tried to keep her face placid while Mom lit into Principal Reed.

"If there's a no tolerance policy for this school, why wasn't Amelia Ryder suspended as well?" Mom asked sweetly.

"She's the injured party." His jaw muscle twitched beneath his sallow skin. All the crap over the last twenty-four hours must be giving him one heck of a case of indigestion.

"She only got injured because Kaley dodged Amelia's punch," Mom pointed out. Her saccharine tone must have been annoying him because his eyes squinched.

"It was a slap," he bit out.

"So, you admit Amelia Ryder tried to strike Kaley?" Mom didn't quite have her "A-HA!" reporter tone, but it was pretty darn close.

"You're twisting my words." Principal Reed's voice grew louder.

"But what you're saying is Kaley didn't raise a hand, Amelia did, and now you're suspending Kaley." Mom held up her copy of the Student Handbook with the applicable sub paragraph highlighted. "It also sounds like you totally ignored any witnesses to the situation."

"Sometimes, I don't have time to take a formal statement from every student." A bright red blush flowed past his collar and necktie and all the way up to the really bad toupee he thought hid his baldness.

"Really?" Mom leaned forward. "Because we had an interesting visit from Sheriff Birkheimer early this morning, and it sounds like he's doing a more thorough investigation into the incident between the girls than you are. I'm sure the voters in Holmes County will be interested in how you handle things at the high school with both the election coming up in a couple of weeks and your contract ending at the end of the school year." She finished with her faux charming smile, the one she wore to the various church pancake dinners.

Principal Reed glared at her for a long time before he finally said, "What do you want me to do?"

"Both girls get off with a warning." Mom shrugged. "Amelia did enough damage to herself. I hope she learned her lesson."

His nostrils flared as he exhaled. "Fine. Kaley, get a hall pass from my secretary—"

"Administrative assistant." Mom stood and shook her head. "Really, Lester? I know we're in rural Ohio, but it is the twenty-first century."

Luckily, superpowers weren't a real thing among Normals. Otherwise, Mom would have been crispy fried by Principal Reed's laser vision from the ugly look he gave her.

"Get a hall pass from Mrs. Snyder, Kaley, and get to class."

"Thank you, Lester." Mom grinned as she slung her bag over her shoulder. "See you at next month's school board meeting!" Of course, she'd have a little talk with the superintendent, possibly even on the record, about Principal Reed's inability to equitably adhere to the school's rules.

When Kaley and Mom walked out of the administration

office with the hall pass, Mom murmured, "Don't you dare do a fist pump."

"I wasn't going to," Kaley protested, though the thought had crossed her mind.

"Mmm-hmmm."

Ignoring Mom's skepticism, Kaley said, "What are we going to do if that apparition goes back to the hospital?"

"For right now, you're not doing a thing." Mom stopped in the hallway and stared at her. "You are going to class, and you're going to cheerleading practice, and you're keeping your nose clean. If Jennifer or Madison give you any grief, you call me."

"But—"

"No 'but's, young lady," Mom said sternly before she pulled Kaley in a tight hug. "Just watch your back here. Let me worry about our culprit."

Mom released Kaley and stalked toward the main entrance. Kaley watched Mom until she disappeared from sight.

Kirsten was right. This was becoming quite personal. They should have mentioned the possibility of the Ryders hiring an eclectic to Sheriff Birkheimer. He could have done some quiet checking.

Kaley sighed, checked the time on her phone, and headed for her locker. For now, she needed to worry about the physics quiz she hadn't bothered studying for.

When Kaley walked into the girls' locker room at the end of the day, Mandy Jenkins grinned at her. She'd been on the receiving end of Amelia's crap a lot more often than Kaley had been.

"Glad to see the suspension didn't stick," Mandy said.

"Truth wills out," Kaley replied. They both looked at Jennifer and Madison in the corner, murmuring to each other and shooting Kaley ugly, pointed looks.

Before they were stupid enough to say or do anything, Hope Stillwell, Kirsten, and a couple of other girls' from the varsity basketball team entered the locker room.

"Hey, I thought conditioning had been cancelled again," Kaley said to her sister. "Ms. Park wasn't in health class today. The rumor mill says her mom's still in CCU."

Kirsten shrugged. "We all had our stuff with us, so we figured we'd get in some cardio." She glanced at Jennifer and Madison. Hope made a point of using the bench next to the two cheerleaders. Not even the boys messed with Hope. She was six feet tall and nearly as strong as Donny from working on her parents' farm. If that wasn't enough to dissuade idiots, there were her three older brothers, all of them career marines.

Any problems? Kirsten asked silently.

Not yet. Kaley grinned. *The pyramid has yet to be formed.*

Ms. Cross charged into the locker room. "Wilson!" She stopped abruptly when she realized there were more girls than just the cheer squad. "What are you girls doing in here?"

Hope rose to her full height, which was a foot taller than the coach. "With Coach Park dealing with her mother's health, we're doing our own cardio."

Kaley bit her lower lip to keep from laughing at the consternation on Ms. Cross's face. She couldn't argue with Hope, especially since the West Holmes girls' team would be making another run for the state finals this year. On the other hand, she couldn't say anything nasty to Kaley without a ton of witnesses.

Ms. Cross finally settled on saying, "Very well. Cheer squad out on the field in five." She pivoted and marched out of the girls' locker room.

"Honestly, I think things will be much more pleasant around here while a certain someone is laid up," Mandy murmured.

"Everything at West Holmes will be more pleasant without the self-appointed queen," Hope added.

While a couple of other girls snickered at their comments, Kaley exchanged a guilty look with Kirsten. *If Amelia getting injured is my fault, even indirectly—*

It's not. Kirsten scowled. *She shouldn't have tried to hit you. It's the Threefold Law in action. We need to find the person controlling the specter. You seem to be the focus. At least for now. We need to use that.*

Kaley knelt to tie her shoes. Despite her sister's words, she couldn't help the nagging sense that whoever was behind the chaos was right under her nose.

Chapter 13

Kirsten's phone buzzed as she headed out to the student parking lot. Running a couple of miles with Hope and the others plus a hot shower had cleared her head. Enough to realize if the culprit wasn't an eclectic screwing with Kaley, then it had to be someone they knew.

But Kirsten's money was still on an eclectic.

She pulled her phone from the front pocket of her jeans and checked the number. It wasn't one she recognized, but she read the text anyway.

This is Sheriff Birkheimer. Would you mind giving me a call? I have a favor to ask.

That was a little weird. But if Jimmy was using his title, he may have learned something about the specter. She tossed her exercise gear into the trunk before she leaned against the bumper and thumbed the call icon.

The line rang twice. The sheriff's crisp business voice said, "Birkheimer here. Thanks for calling me back, Kirsten."

"This isn't an official call, is it?"

His exhale whistled through the receiver. "Not exactly, but sort of." The background noise died. "I'm at the hospital. Tina had to go home early because her son is sick. Jo's at work, and Deputy Wolford has to sleep sometime."

"And Mom's at work, too, which leaves me as the only competent semi-adult witch, who isn't a cheerleader or a suspect, for you to call on for assistance." It was probably a good thing he couldn't see her grin.

"I'm afraid so," he said. "You up for it? Or is high school mean girl shit going to get in the way?"

"I'll do it. I've got nothing against Amelia."

"Does that mean Kaley does?" Wow, he wasn't going to let this go, was he?

"No, it means Amelia doesn't consider bookworm jocks like me competition for boys' attention, so she pretty much leaves me alone. But that damn specter, or whatever it really is, tried to kill me, so I'm saying I'm in for whatever help you need."

"Thanks, Kirsten. I appreciate your help. How soon can you get here?"

For some reason, the thought of Uncle Jimmy trusting her gave her a pleased feeling. Plus, it would give her a chance to question Amelia about hiring an eclectic to frame Kaley. The head cheerleader would be on some pretty good painkillers after her surgery and probably less likely to keep any lies straight.

"I'm about to leave school." Kirsten counted the times in her head. "Let me call Mom so she knows where I'm at and grab a burger. I'll be there in twenty minutes unless a whitetail runs into me."

Uncle Jimmy chuckled. "I'll see you when you get here. Thanks again."

She shoved her phone back into her pocket and concentrated. *Kaley?*

Yeah. Kaley's disgust felt like wading through a manure spreader.

I need to do a favor for Uncle Jimmy. Can you catch a ride home with Donny?

Disbelief beat Kaley's actual words to Kirsten. *After he accused me of deliberately knee-capping Amelia this morning?*

He was doing his job. Kirsten wasn't sure revealing the truth to her twin was such a good idea at the moment. At least, not all of it. *And I want him on our side when Mr. Ryder sics his attorneys on Mom and Dad.*

Crap. I didn't think of that. Kaley was quiet for a few seconds, her concentration split. She was probably checking with Donny, which she confirmed with, *Yeah, I can catch a ride with him.*

Kirsten released the link with her sister and climbed into the driver seat of Mom's car. If she ended up at an out-of-side university, she would definitely need some wheels if she didn't go to school someplace with a good public transportation system. Even though she'd put nearly everything she made working for Aunt Jo into savings, the amount wouldn't buy anything decent. Nor could she rely on Dad when things invariably broke beyond flat tires and broken wiper blades.

She texted Mom with the update. Mom replied with "Be careful."

Kirsten backed out of her parking spot and drove toward the exit. Yep, once she dealt with this so-called specter, she needed to rethink her freshman college budget.

Inside one of the hospital's elevators, Kirsten punched the button for the floor Uncle Jimmy had texted her. The salt was a comforting weight in her backpack while the car carried her upward. When the doors slid open, he sat in the waiting room, flipping through a magazine. He placed the copy of *Good House-keeping* in the rack next to his chair when he spotted her.

"I thought you were more of a *Guns & Ammo* guy." She gestured at the top of the rack where most of the outdoor lifestyle magazines stood.

Jimmy glanced at the ones she indicated. "Already read those at home." He turned back to her. "Besides, I need to learn how to pluck my brows properly if I'm going to attract the right guy."

She laughed at the idea of him plucking his bushy black brows.

He pursed his lips and exhaled. "Just to warn you Amelia's dad is back there."

Kirsten shook her head. "That means you seriously owe me."

Jimmy reached into his uniform jacket pocket and handed her a couple of bills. "Money for pop and snacks work?"

"It's a start." She turned and smoothed the paper currency so the machines would accept it. Once she had an orange pop and a bag of pretzels, she faced Jimmy again. "You have told the staff and her parents who's watching Amelia for the next few hours, haven't you?"

"No," he admitted. "I didn't want to give Ryder a chance to throw a fit."

"Smart move." She slung her backpack off her shoulder and stashed her snacks inside.

Together, Kirsten and Jimmy walked down the corridor to Amelia's room. He knocked when they reached the right door. A chair and a tiny table sat in the corridor.

Kirsten breathed a sigh of relief. At least, Jimmy didn't expect her to stay inside the other teen's room for the full time.

A masculine voice rumbled, "Come in."

Kirsten followed Jimmy inside the room. Her eyes were

immediately drawn to Amelia. Without her makeup, she looked like a scared little girl. A scared little girl who was having trouble focusing on Kirsten.

However, Mr. Ryder jumped to his feet, red fury infusing his face. "What the hell is she doing here?"

"After last night, I need someone here to watch your daughter—"

"Get another deputy!"

"Keep you voice down," Kirsten hissed. "This is a hospital, and your daughter just had surgery."

"Why, you little—"

"Do not finish that statement, Ryder," Jimmy warned. "Let's take this outside." When Mr. Ryder didn't move, Jimmy growled, "Now. Or I arrest you for obstruction of justice."

That threat got Mr. Ryder to stalk out of the hospital room. Jimmy and Kirsten followed him out. Amelia didn't say a word because she'd fallen back to sleep.

Out in the hallway, Mr. Ryder whirled to face Jimmy. "After what her sister did—" Mr. Ryder started to say through gritted teeth.

"Your daughter assaulted Kaley Wilson. You threatened to get the cheerleading coach fired if she didn't make Amelia head cheerleader for this school year." Jimmy acted perfectly calm as he ticked off the issues. "Then you threatened Coach Cross's job again after Amelia hurt herself during her assault of Kaley. And now, I've got a specter floating around harassing citizens."

Mr. Ryder glared at Kirsten. "I can guess who's controlling it."

Jimmy rested his hands on his utility belt. "And if I go digging some more, am I going to find out you hired another witch to harass the Wilson twins, Rose Gleason, and the kids Kaley babysits?"

Kirsten sucked in a breath. So much for her chance at subtly asking Amelia.

Mr. Ryder's face turned beet red. "My lawyer will be in touch with you about your allegations."

Interesting. He didn't deny the involvement of an eclectic. Kirsten mentally noted the questions she needed to ask Amelia when she woke up.

Jimmy shrugged. "He's more than welcome to. In the meantime, this specter seems focused on people associated with Kaley Wilson. I need someone up here I can trust and with experience in the craft to keep an eye on Amelia if this specter shows up at the hospital again tonight."

"Deputy Wolford—"

Jimmy seemed determined not to let Mr. Ryder finish a sentence. "Julia's got to sleep sometime. So do I. But surely you don't want to leave Amelia unprotected, do you?"

The red drained from Mr. Ryder. "You can't be seriously about leaving her—" He jabbed his right index finger in Kirsten's direction. "—here to watch my daughter."

"I'm the only experienced witch available in town at the moment," Kirsten said. "But if you want call your eclectic, I'll leave once they arrive."

"Fine," Mr. Ryder snapped. "I'll call her." He pulled his phone out of his jacket pocket.

"And I'll need her name and number." Jimmy smiled.

Kirsten bit her lip to keep from laughing. If looks could kill, Jimmy would be a pile of guts on the hospital's pristine floor. But it did answer the question of whether Mr. Ryder had an eclectic in his employ.

Mr. Ryder showed Jimmy the contact information, and the sheriff made a note on his own phone.

"Catherine Kowalski," Jimmy muttered. "You know her, Kirsten?"

She shook her head. "But that doesn't mean anything. I'm pretty young by witch standards. Aunt Jo might."

"All right." Jimmy gestured for Mr. Ryder to make the call.

Amelia's father walked away from both them and the nurses' station. He didn't look pleased as he spoke, but then freelance eclectics weren't cheap.

"Can you hear what he's saying?" Jimmy murmured.

Kirsten leaned closer to the sheriff and whispered, "I think you have me mistaken for a were or a vamp."

He grinned. "Maybe I need to recruit Kaley's buddy Donny. What's the deal with those two? They spend a lot of time together for a couple who aren't dating."

"I don't know." Kirsten rolled her eyes. "I can't figure them out either."

Mr. Ryder stomped back over to them. "She can't be here until eight tonight."

Jimmy nodded. "How late can your eclectic stay?"

"Why am I paying to guard my daughter?" Red climbed Mr. Ryder's face again.

"Because I don't have a supernatural in the sheriff's department, the police department doesn't either, and you're throwing a fit about the one volunteer I could scrounge." Jimmy shook his head. "You can't have it both ways, Art."

Mr. Ryder glared at Jimmy for a long time before he said, "We'll do it your way." His attention turned to Kirsten. "But if anything happens to Amelia—"

"If something happens to her after I leave, I'll know I was set up," Kirsten said evenly.

"You watch your mouth, little girl," Mr. Ryder snarled.

"That's enough from both of you," Jimmy ordered. "Ryder tell your daughter good night, and then you need to leave. But if you're staying until your eclectic arrives, I'm sending Kirsten home."

The sheriff's threat seemed to knock some sense into the man. He entered Amelia's hospital room. He and Amelia spoke though Kirsten couldn't hear what they said.

Mr. Ryder stalked out of the room and headed toward the elevator without a word to Jimmy or Kirsten.

"Wow. Talk about entitled," she murmured.

"Some people love being the giant fish in the teeny, tiny pond," Jimmy said.

"Hallelujah," the nurse grumbled as she walked into Amelia's room.

"I'd prefer you stay in there with her, but if she gives you a hard time, then . . ." Jimmy waved at the chair and table by the doorway.

"I think I can handle a cheerleader on heavy-duty painkillers." Kirsten grinned.

"Speaking from experience?" he teased.

She shrugged. "Only when Kaley had her wisdom teeth pulled."

He sobered. "Call me if you need anything, if Ryder returns, or—"

"This Catherine won't do anything if she wants to continue practicing in Ohio. I'll text Aunt Jo whether she knows this woman." She swung her backpack off her shoulder. "Not to mention I came prepared."

"Thanks, Kirsten." He patted her shoulder. "I owe you one."

"And I'll collect." She grinned.

He sauntered in the direction of the elevators. Kirsten sucked in a deep breath and entered Amelia's room. The nurse was removing her gloves.

"You're a good person for staying with your friend," she said as she tossed them into the trash.

"Were you here last night?" Kirsten asked.

"No, it was my day off." The nurse pressed the button to dispense hand sanitizer. "Though I heard about the ghost dog through the hospital grapevine. I have half a mind to ask your Aunt Jo to whip up one of her protective charms for me."

"As long as you stay away from my sister, you should be fine. This thing seems to be attracted to anyone who associates with her." Kirsten smiled. Maybe she could discover more about what people had seen last night. She followed the nurse back out into the hallway and to the nurses' station. "Are there any eyewitnesses from last night who are on duty tonight? Every scrap of information could help us figure out what triggered this specter."

"Just a second." The nurse held up her index finger before she shuffled through some papers. "Leslie Brigham and Cynthia Cross had the eleven to seven shift for this ward last night. They both are working tonight, too."

"Thanks." Kirsten pulled out her phone and made notes of the names.

The nurse propped her fists on her hips. "You think the ghost dog might go after the other cheerleaders?"

Kirsten shoved her phone back into her jeans pockets. "Like I said, it seems to be focused on my sister Kaley and people she knows so it's possible—"

At the far of the corridor, a flash of light caught Kirsten's attention. The specter padded around the corner. This time, she had no doubt. It took the shape of a ghostly blue version of Donny in his coyote form.

Chapter 14

Kaley slid into the passenger seat of Donny's antique sedan. He tossed his gym bag in the backseat and climbed into the car.

"Sorry you didn't get to take the day off after all." He grinned.

"I think the suspension would have been better than the cold shoulder I was getting at practice," she grumbled.

"Yeah, I noticed." He stuck his key in the ignition and twisted. The engine roared to life. He checked his mirrors before he backed out of his parking spot.

Kaley snorted. "I'm sure the entire football team did."

Donny glanced at her before pressing the accelerator. "You going to quit?"

"Hell, no!"

"Good," he murmured.

"Why?"

"Because humans think they're above animals, but they really aren't." He flipped the turn signal and braked at the end of the school's drive. "You quit, and that's like blood in the water to Amelia and her cronies."

Kaley sighed and leaned her head against the window. The cool glass felt good against her heated skin. "I'm beginning to see why Kirsten wants to leave Millersburg so bad."

"Kirsten wants to leave?" He stared at Kaley as he made the turn onto the state highway. A horn blared. He jerked the steering wheel, and the sedan whipped back into the correct lane, barely missing the empty logging truck.

Kaley bit her bottom lip to keep from laughing. She felt bad for Donny, but he needed to get up the nerve to ask Kirsten out himself. Getting into the middle of things would be the best way to ruin her relationship with both her best friend and her sister.

Donny cleared his throat. "Where's she planning on going to school?"

"She wants to go out of state." Kaley straightened in her seat. "A lot of it depends on getting a scholarship or two. Hope's a shoo-in for getting an athletic one because of her height."

"She and Kirsten should be going for academic scholarships," Donny said. "If they get hurt on the court, poof! No more scholarship."

"All I can tell you is wherever she goes, it will be somewhere I don't." She couldn't stop the hurt in her voice.

"You know she loves you."

"But she thinks she lives under my shadow."

"It's not uncommon in identical twins for one to be more extroverted than their sibling," Donny said.

"Says the only child," Kaley shot back.

And immediately regretted her words.

"Oh, Goddess, I'm sorry, Donny," she said. "That was an awful thing for me to say."

"I keep defending you," he said. "I tell everyone you're not a stuck-up bitch like Amelia. You're not even worried about that damn specter. No, you're whining because you're identical twin sister, and I'd like to point out you dyed your freaking hair so you wouldn't look quite as much like her, wants to go to a different school than you."

Kaley opened her mouth to yell at him.

And promptly shut it. Maybe he was right. Maybe the distance between her and Kirsten was partly her fault.

"So what do I do?" she asked quietly.

"I don't have any siblings so how the hell would I know?" he snapped.

"Look, you're right," she said. "I'm being a bitch. Can we please call a truce before we stop being friends?"

He glanced at her before he blew out a deep breath. "Fine." After a long pause, he said, "Have you checked on Miz Rose since Monday?"

"Oh, crap," she muttered. "I need to go over to her house tonight and refresh her protective charms."

"What do you mean refresh her charms?" Donny asked.

"Kirsten and I had to do some substitutions." She pulled out her phone to check the weather since her sister had Mom's car. Last thing she wanted to do was miss school, and therefore Friday night's football game, because she made herself sick walking home in the rain.

"I can take you over," Donny said.

"You don't have to," she replied.

"Just because I got mad at you for saying something shitty doesn't mean our friendship is over, Drama Queen." He grinned. "I care about Miz Rose, too."

The familiar insult made her feel a little better. "I still need to swing by our house to get some supplies."

However, Dad's truck already sat in the drive when Donny braked in front of their house. Surely, her parents wouldn't get uptight about her and Donny checking on Miz Rose.

Kaley opened the front door, only to be greeted with the sounds of Mom and Dad yelling in the back of the house. They rarely fought, but after Dad's comments at dinner last night, maybe things weren't as settled as she thought.

"Are you trying to get our daughters killed?" Dad roared.

Kaley glanced at Donny. "So much for grabbing supplies and leaving."

He smirked. "I think it's safe for us to hit the kitchen. Your mom just told your dad to shut up because we walked in."

Oh geez. Was this about the favor Jimmy wanted Kirsten to do?

Kaley and Donny walked into the kitchen. Mom and Dad looked everywhere but at each other. Their faces were bright pink. Mom shielded her emotions, but Dad couldn't, and he was pissed as hell.

"We'll be out of your hair in a minute." Kaley strode over to Mom's herb cupboard. "I need to go down to Miz Rose's house to reinforce the protection spells Kirsten and I laid on Monday."

From the spike in Dad's anger, he and Mom were definitely arguing about her twin.

"Are you going with her, Donny?" Dad asked.

"I planned on it," Donny answered. "More rain's expected, and Kirsten doesn't need to be walking home in it." He shrugged. "Unless you want to drive her."

"No, that's fine," Mom said. "Why don't you stay for supper tonight? We owe you for giving the girls a ride home the last couple of nights."

"That sounds great." The were grinned.

Kaley focused on putting the right herbs in plastic bags. Mom's invitation was yet another reminder Donny didn't have the home life she did. Even with his mom working two jobs and Donny helping on various farms during the summer, they had trouble making ends meet at times. In fact, getting Donny's beater running was part of the reason they hadn't worked on the '69 for the last two years.

"Any last minute tips, Mom?" Kaley asked as she exchanged her homework materials for the baggies filled with herbs and dragon's blood resin in her backpack.

"You know how to do a basic protection spell." Mom pursed her lips.

Kaley slung her backpack over her shoulders. "Then why don't you and Dad trust that Kirsten knows how to take care of herself, too?"

"We do, honey," Dad said. "It's just that—"

"You still think of us as little girls." Kaley shook her head. "What are you going to do in two years when we're at college? Put tracking collars and body cams on us?"

"It crossed my mind," Dad said dryly.

"Ethan!" Mom looked totally appalled.

"I wasn't actually going to do it," Dad retorted.

"I feel sorry for whoever dates your daughters," Donny said.

Kaley, Mom, and Dad stared at Donny, but he just snickered. Kaley dragged him out of the house before Dad followed through with his previous threat to neuter her best friend.

Chapter 15

The nurse started to turn to see what Kirsten was staring at, but she grabbed the older woman's arm.

"It's behind me, isn't it?" the nurse whispered. Her arm shook though her voice didn't.

"Don't turn around." Kirsten slid her phone out of her jeans pocket. "Go behind the nurses' desk and call Sheriff Birkheimer. My PIN is four-five-two-nine, and his personal cell number is listed under 'Uncle Jimmy.'"

"I can't leave you by yourself," the nurse protested, but she took the phone.

Kirsten smiled. "That thing is the reason I'm here. I'm the bait."

She gave the nurse a slight push, and the older woman scampered around the high counter of the nurses' station. Meanwhile, the specter paused at the end of the corridor. Did it remember its tussle here with Deputy Wolford last night? Or its encounters with the sisters?

Kirsten clenched her teeth. She had the salt canister in her backpack, but she'd left her water bottle in the car. It was empty, but she should have brought the bottle with her and filled it in the public bathroom.

Wait, she still carried the pop can courtesy of Jimmy. Kirsten slowly knelt on the floor and unzipped her backpack, keeping her eye on the specter as she did so. She cracked open the can of orange pop and poured it on the floor. Next came the salt. She pried open the spout and dumped a healthy amount in the puddle of pop before she shoved the canister back into her backpack.

The specter hadn't moved. It simply watched her. Kirsten kicked aside her backpack. She sucked in a deep breath. The sharp odor of a thunderstorm filled the corridor. Ozone. Donny wasn't full of crap after all. Kirsten concentrated and gestured. The sugary, salty liquid swirled and rose into the air.

The specter growled. It must have recognized the potential threat.

"I won't hurt you if you leave," she said.

It took a hesitant step closer toward her.

"I'm not going to let you hurt anyone else." She also took a step forward. In the background, the nurse's voice frantically told someone the blue dog ghost was back.

The specter's attention focused on the hospital room on Kirsten's left. Amelia's room.

"The cheerleader has already hurt herself over her own actions. She doesn't need you inflicting more injuries on her."

The specter crouched and launched itself toward Kirsten. She spun the orange pop into a lasso and looped it around the midriff of the specter. It howled, but the cry sounded more like pain than a warning or anger. Maybe the extra acid in the pop did more to it than plain salt water.

Kirsten sidestepped the specter and yanked on her orange pop lasso. It passed through the specter. The beast didn't dissolve. However, it howled again, and its appearance became less distinct. A vague canine shape, but not the spitting image of Donny's second form.

It shook itself, and it shed blue sparks like drops of water.

Kirsten definitely picked up the sense it was furious with her. More likely because she was between it and Amelia, not because of the effect of the salty orange soda.

The specter growled and charged toward her again. Kirsten spun the orange pop into four tendrils. She snapped the mixture whips at the specter. Each strike made its form blur more until it was a blue blob.

She dodged to the side as it passed. The blob slowed and bobbed in the air. A low growl came from the specter.

It was enough of a warning. Kirsten spun the liquid into a disk in front of her an instant before the blob rushed toward her. The specter shrieked when it slammed into the salty liquid. The force knocked her down, and she lost her concentration as she slammed backside first on the floor. Orange pop splashed on her, the linoleum, the walls, and the ceiling. However, the specter dissolved and disappeared.

Kirsten sat upright and frowned. The power of the specter felt more like witch magick instead of ghost energy. Were they dealing with a dead witch?

"Honey, are you okay?" The nurse she'd given her phone to peered over the high countertop of the nurses' station. Two other nurses gazed wide-eyed at her.

"Just sticky." Kirsten grimaced at the sugary liquid soaking her shirt and dripping from her hair. "Do you have a pitcher or something I can use to clean up the mess I made?"

"Sure." The first nurse disappeared while the other two continue to stare at Kirsten lying in a puddle of orange pop.

Mom and Dad always emphasized Kirsten and Kaley shouldn't use their powers in public, even after the Rainier Outing. Not all the Normals were as open-minded as their friends and most of Dad's family. From the way the nurses stared at

Kirsten, she understood some of Dad's worry from the other night. The ladies were making her damn uncomfortable with their fear.

"Here we go." The first nurse charged back toward Kirsten with a huge plastic patient cup in her hands, but she stopped at the edge of the orange splotches. "Where do I need to put it?"

"Just hold it right there, please." Kirsten closed her eyes and focused on the liquid around her. She pulled the droplets together, but it was harder to hold with all the particles suspended in it. People didn't realize how much dust floated in the air and rested on surfaces. Bits that were too small to see with the naked eye.

She poured the liquid she collected into the huge plastic cup the first nurse held. Her eyes blinked open. There was quite a bit of crystalline residue on her shirt, on her skin, and in her hair. She carefully stood. All her joints and muscles seemed to be working, but she was definitely going to be sore in the morning.

"Dang." The first nurse held up the clear plastic cup and gazed at the dirty orange liquid inside. "It would be so much easier to take care of patients and clean my house if I could do that."

"It's not as easy as using a sponge and soap." Kirsten commented.

The pneumatic whine of the elevator doors was followed by loud clattering from the other end of the hallway. Jimmy and three deputies raced around the corner. Each law officer held a steel baton carved with protective symbols.

"Where—" The sheriff looked around wildly.

The first nurse sniffed and inclined her head toward Kirsten. "She already took care of it."

Jimmy pushed his hat back and pinched the bridge of his nose. "Your mother is going to kill me."

Chapter 16

Kaley leaned against the car door and considered Donny's question as he drove down the street. "No, I don't think Mom would kill Uncle Jimmy if the specter hurt Kirsten. But if you're that worried about her, you need to call her."

He stammered and blushed as she expected.

"When are you going to admit you like her?" Kaley said softly.

Donny glanced at her. "She doesn't like me."

"You go out of your way to annoy her." Kaley shook her head. "It's the same crap you did in kindergarten. You need to grow up and treat my sister with a little more respect if you want her attention."

"I do respect her," he protested.

"You know what I mean," she growled.

"So, how do I get Kirsten's attention the right way?"

"Nope, I'm not helping you," Kaley said. "If you haven't figured out how to attract her attention by now, you don't deserve her."

Donny was silent for three blocks before he quietly said, "Is it because I don't like you in that way?"

Kaley glared at him. "Dude, if you have some perverted wish for a ménage with twins, you are barking up the wrong tree."

"That's not the case, and you know it," Donny growled.

Kaley sighed. "You are the only person in the world who treats us like two different people."

"You *are* two different people," he snapped.

"But that's not how most people see me and Kirsten." Kaley's eyes burned. "Not even our parents sometimes. Everyone looks at us like we're a matched set."

"Has it occurred to you that might be why Kirsten wants to leave Millersburg?" Donny said softly.

"Then you need to give her a reason to stay." Kaley swiped at the wetness on her cheeks. "Because I sure as hell can't."

Orange and purple lights twinkled in Miz Rose's windows when Donny parked his car in front of her house.

"You sure you're up to doing this?"

"Yeah," Kaley murmured. "Miz Rose doesn't need the specter to come back and break all her stuff." She grabbed her backpack. "Or at least what's left."

They both got out of the ancient sedan and trudged up the walk. A chill, damp wind and dark clouds threatened to dump more rain on Millersburg. They also spurred Kaley to pick up her pace.

She jogged up the steps to the Victorian and raised her fist to knock. The front door flew open before she could touch the stained mahogany.

"Thank goodness you're here," Miz Rose said breathlessly. "I was about to call Jo. It's back."

"The specter?" Kaley said.

Donny pushed past her and Miz Rose. "Where?"

"In the family room, but Kaley—" Miz Rose grabbed Kaley's right arm as she started to follow Donny. "It's not throwing anything or damaging my belongings. It's acting like an injured animal."

"That could make it even more dangerous." Kaley whirled. "Donny, wait!" When the were paused, she turned back to Miz Rose and handed the older lady her keychain. The steel triquetra shimmered under the entryway light. "Grab your coat and wait for us in Donny's car."

Miz Rose didn't argue. She slung on her coat and tottered out to the sedan. Once she was inside the car, Kaley closed the front door.

"I'm still going first," Donny growled.

"That's fine," she shot back. "But don't yell at me if you get hurt."

They crept down the hallway to the kitchen. Kaley grabbed his shoulder before he entered.

"Do you see any knives out?" she whispered.

Donny peered around the doorjamb and checked the room, even looking at the ceiling and crouching to check under Miz Rose's farmer's table. He slowly straightened and started to shake his head when he froze.

"It's still in the family room." He cocked his head. "It sounds like a little kid crying."

"Let me go in first in case I need to throw up a ward," Kaley whispered.

Donny stared at her a long time, like he wanted to argue, but in the end, he nodded. All his strength and speed meant nothing if the specter had anything in the family room besides pillow fluff.

She crept through the kitchen to the family room doorway.

A chill emanated from the area as if the air conditioner was turned to its lowest setting. However, Donny was so tight against her back she didn't need her varsity jacket to stay warm. She crouched and peered around the doorjamb.

Miz Rose had put several of the undamaged photographs into new frames and hung them on the walls. But it was the soft blue glow from behind the armchair in the far left corner of the room that unnerved Kaley. Now, she could hear the muffled sobbing Donny mentioned.

"What do you smell?" she whispered.

"Ginger." Donny cocked his head and sniffed again before he looked down at her. "It's definitely giving off a ginger scent along with the ozone."

"And before?" Kaley prodded.

He shrugged. "Like I said, just ozone."

Was there another witch in town who was bent on antagonizing the Normals? A dark suspicion filled her. Or was this someone she knew? The only person she could rule out was her twin because the specter had definitely tried to hurt her sister in this same kitchen.

She crept forward, the spell for a ward on the tip of her tongue. The specter didn't react to her presence like it had the first time in Miz Rose's house with threats or actual violence. She eased around the chair. This time, the specter was an amorphous blob on the carpet. It shivered in time to the child-like crying noises.

Kaley reached out a hand, but before she could touch the specter, it abruptly vanished.

Chapter 17

Uncle Jimmy escorted Kirsten to Mom's car.

"I'm fine," she protested. "I can drive home."

"I'm sure you can, but it's best I face the music with your parents for dragging you into this mess." He shook his head. "I just hope your mom doesn't turn me into a newt."

Kirsten stopped and stared at him. "You do know we really can't do stuff like that, don't you?"

"Okay, maybe not turn me into a newt," Uncle Jimmy conceded. "But you have to admit she could launch a fireball up my ass."

"Well, yeah, she could." Kirsten giggled. "Sometimes, I think Dad wishes he was a fire witch."

"No, kiddo, he wishes he was a water witch like you."

Uncle Jimmy's statement clicked everything together about why Dad strongly nudged her to apply for the Ohio State veterinarian program. While her healing abilities weren't on par with most other water witches, she'd been able to sense what was wrong with animals when she hung out at Dad's clinic during summer vacations. While she loved and respected Dad, she wasn't sure she wanted to follow in his footsteps.

She and Uncle Jimmy continued to Mom's car, and she reluctantly gave him the keys. At least, he was nice enough to pick up dinner for her on the way home.

Teller wound around Kirsten's ankles in a figure-eight pattern between delicately taking the bites of hamburger she slipped him under the table. Penn perched on the kitchen counter and watched Mom, Dad, and Uncle Jimmy argue. She had the distinct impression the humans thoroughly amused her sister's cat.

"I can't believe you deliberately put my daughter in danger," Dad hollered.

"Kirsten handled herself just fine," Uncle Jimmy shot back. "Better than some supernatural enforcers I know. She kept her head in a crisis and prevented that damn specter from hurting any of the patients or staff. And that's with salt and a can of pop. With a little training, she could—"

"I don't want my daughter to become an enforcer!" Mom interrupted. "Things in the world are crazy enough for supernaturals without painting a target on her back!"

"That's not your decision, Mom," Kirsten said quietly.

The three adults slowly turned to stare at her. Uncle Jimmy smirked. Dad frowned. Mom's face turned nearly scarlet.

"I'm not giving you lip," Kirsten added in the same low even tone. "But my career isn't your choice, just as yours wasn't Grandma's. Frankly, it felt good helping the nurses protect the patients."

"You have no idea of what you're dealing with," Mom snapped.

"It's not a specter," Kirsten said before she popped a fry into her mouth.

"You sure?" Uncle Jimmy asked at the same time as Dad said, "What is it?"

She swallowed her fry. "Fairly sure. At first, the thing looked exactly like Donny in his coyote form, it was very resistant to the salt I used, and there was a definite odor of ozone before I injured it."

"It's a spell?" Mom's brows scrunched together the way they always did when she was faced with a puzzle whether mundane or magickal.

"If it is, it's more than just a spell." Kirsten swirled another fry through her ketchup.

"You absolutely sure it wasn't fairy?" Uncle Jimmy asked.

Mom winced at his racial slur.

"Oh, yeah, I would so sling spells at a fae and blow up the hospital." Sarcasm dripped from Kirsten's voice, but after he'd said how good she'd done, his comment was a little insulting.

"Kirsten." Dad frowned at her.

"I'm sorry, Uncle Jimmy." Kirsten lifted her chin. "But I resent being treated like I'd be stupid enough to cross the streams."

Her phone jingled with the tune to Kaley's favorite boy band. Kirsten pulled the sticky device from her pocket. At least, it was still working after getting doused in salty orange pop. And it was super serious if her twin was calling instead of texting.

Mom and Dad stared at Kirsten like she was being rude for answering the damn thing, which only irritated her more.

"What do you need, Kaley?" she bit out.

"Who peed in your Cheerios?" Kaley shot back.

"Sorry." Kirsten took a sip of her soda, swallowed, and said more calmly, "What do you need?"

"Are you still at the hospital?"

"No, I'm currently being treated like a baby by our parents after I kept the specter from attacking Amelia." Kirsten reached for a fry. "By the way, I don't think it's a specter."

"Yeah, Donny and I came to the same conclusion."

Kirsten straightened in her chair. "Wait, are you saying you saw it tonight?"

"Yeah," Kaley said. "Donny drove me over to Miz Rose's place to redo the wards. Make 'em a little more permanent. It showed up here, except it looked like a blue blob again, and it cried like it was injured. Donny said it smelled like ozone and ginger, but it didn't hurt Miz Rose or even try to attack us."

"That confirms my suspicion a spell's animating this thing." Kirsten popped the fry in her mouth. "It must have gone back to Miz Rose's because our quick and dirty protection spell is failing."

"That's what we think, too." Kaley sighed. "Let me do the permanent wards, and we'll compare notes when I get home."

A male voice rumbled in the background.

Kaley groaned. "Okay, fine. When Donny and I get home."

"See you in a bit." Kirsten thumbed the icon to end the call.

"Is Kaley all right?" Dad said at the same time Mom blurted, "It showed up at Rose's again?"

Uncle Jimmy wisely remained silent.

"Yeah, but I must have injured it pretty good." Kirsten reached for another fry. "Kirsten said it was a blue blob again, and it was crying."

"Is Rose all right?" Concern for the elderly woman was written all over Mom's face.

"Miz Rose is fine, just upset it came back." Kirsten chewed her fry while Mom peppered her with questions.

"Rach, calm down and let the girl answer," Uncle Jimmy said.

Kirsten swallowed her fry. "Can we wait until Kaley and Donny get back, please? We can all discuss this at the same time. You might want to call Aunt Jo because if Kaley and I are right, we might have a rogue witch on our hands."

Chapter 18

When Kaley entered the kitchen, she understood the saying about cutting the tension with a knife. Behind her, Donny emitted a low growl from deep in his chest.

Aunt Jo and Uncle Jimmy sat on one side of the kitchen table. Dad and Kirsten sat on the other side. Mom, however, paced like a caged animal, and there was a hint of burning leaves in the air.

Mom eyed Kaley and Donny before she turned to Kirsten. Her twin twirled a spoon through a large dish of Dad's tin roof. Whatever the hell was going on had to be bad if Kirsten was eating ice cream this close to the start of basketball season.

"You want to go first, or you want me to?" Kirsten said.

Kaley shrugged. "You ran into it first tonight. Let me grab a notebook so we can draw the timeline."

At her sister's nod, Kaley slid her backpack from her shoulders and took the chair at the end of the table. She pulled out her history notebook and opened it to the clean pages in the back. After she retrieved her favorite gel pens from the side pocket, she said, "Go."

Kirsten relayed her encounter at the hospital, including the specter's resemblance to Donny's werecoyote form. All the adults stared at him.

Donny held up his hands. "I was at school all day, football

practice this afternoon, and with Kaley over at Miz Rose's. It couldn't have been me at the hospital."

Kaley detailed the events this evening at Miz Rose's. Dad and Uncle Jimmy looked confused, but Mom and Jo wore concerned expressions.

"Honey, please tell me you properly reinforced the protective warding at Rose's house before you came home," Mom said.

"Yes," Kaley snapped. "How could you think I'd let that thing hurt Miz Rose?"

"And you smelled ozone again at Rose's house tonight?" Mom asked Donny.

He nodded. "Tonight was the first time I picked up ginger from the specter."

"I think we can all agree it's definitely not a specter," Jo said.

"What's the connection though?" Uncle Jimmy asked.

"Let's go back and start from the beginning," Dad suggested.

"The specter first showed up at Rose's over the weekend, but it was first visible to the girls on Monday," Jo said.

"Rose didn't actually see anything?" Mom asked.

"According to her at the coffee shop on Monday, no." Jo turned to Kaley. "Did she say anything Monday or tonight about seeing it?"

"She said it was invisible to her when Kirsten and I were there on Monday." Kaley marked it on her timeline. "But she could see it tonight, and she saw the same blue blob Donny and I did." She switched to her red pen for that note.

"Sounds like it was becoming more powerful before Kirsten hurt it at the hospital tonight," Uncle Jimmy ventured.

"And it seems to be focused on Kaley . . ." Kirsten frowned at her twin. "You didn't actually hurt it. I played offense and you played defense on Monday."

Kaley rolled her eyes. "Do you have to put everything in sports terms?"

"Monday night, you saw it out at the Eislers' place . . ." Kirsten had the same expression of concentration she had when she worked on calculus problems. "Donny saw it, too, in the woods, but it didn't do anything to either of you."

"Except for the knives and glass at Miz Rose's on Monday." Kaley held up her arms to display her bandages for the cuts.

"But not on Tuesday, which is also when Amelia busted her knee while trying to smack you," Donny pointed out.

"Are you saying this thing is protective of Kaley?" Dad asked.

A shiver ran down her spine. "So we have a potential rogue witch with an obsession with teenage cheerleaders? That's not creepy at all, Dad."

"Not an obsession," Kirsten mused. "Maybe a crush? Or admiration? Maybe our witch isn't even doing it consciously. Maybe they look up to their babysitter."

Kaley shook her head. "Are you kidding me? Noah and Mila can't possibly be doing this. They both have enough trouble doing a basic warding spell."

"What if it's Tina?" Uncle Jimmy asked. "She wasn't at the hospital the two times this specter thing showed up there."

"She wasn't home when it showed up at their mobile home last night," Jo said. "And the specter chased us when we were on our way to escort Kaley home."

"Crap," Mom muttered. "It could be Tina. Ken was supposed to have the kids over the holiday weekend when this all started, but he decided to go camping with his new girlfriend instead. Tina was pissed as heck. And she depends on Kaley a lot for watching her kids."

"I think I need to have a little talk with Ms. Eisler," Uncle Jimmy proclaimed.

"You're not going out there without me," Mom declared.

"Do you really think Tina would try to hurt Jimmy?" Dad asked.

"Not on purpose if our so-called specter is a subconscious manifestation of her anger," Mom replied.

Uncle Jimmy pushed to feet. "Rachel, if you don't mind, I'd like to get this settled tonight. One way or the other before Art Ryder gets a whiff of our suspicions. I don't trust him not to sic his eclectic on Tina after what happened to his daughter."

"Ryder has an eclectic?" Pink flushed Jo's cheeks.

"A Catherine Kowalski." Uncle Jimmy said. "You know her?"

Jo's face turned from pink to red, and Kaley shook with the wave of fury coming off their aunt. "She's a nasty piece of work. She was exiled from the Toledo coven for performing blood magick using sacrifices."

Kaley exchanged looks with Kirsten. "The Threefold Law?"

"It would explain how Amelia messed up her knee so bad," Kirsten replied. "You're really going to have watch your back when Amelia returns to school if her dad's eclectic is giving her hexes to use on people she doesn't like."

The adults stared at them like they were crazy, but Donny snickered.

"This isn't funny," Jo snapped.

"Sorry to disagree, Miz Jo," he answered. "But my mom says if a Normal or a were is dumb enough to mess with magick, then they deserve what they get." He shrugged. "Of course, she was referring to my dumbass sire, but it applies to Amelia just as equally."

Uncle Jimmy cleared his throat. "Rachel, we need to get going."

Mom nodded and crossed to the wall peg holding her coat. "Don't wait up for me."

She and Uncle Jimmy left, and Dad sighed.

"I guess I'm making dinner tonight." He pushed to his feet. "Do you want anything more to eat, Kirsten?"

"Yes, please," she said.

"Let me wash up and I'll help." Donny finally took off his coat and hung it up.

Kaley stared at her timeline. It fit Uncle Jimmy's suspicions, but something about it gnawed on her instinct.

What's wrong? Kirsten asked.

Something isn't fitting. Kaley shook her head and eyed her twin. *Why was the specter mimicking Donny? Tina's never seen him in coyote form.*

Chapter 19

Her sister's questioned bothered Kirsten the rest of the night. Maybe, because it involved the werecoyote. He'd irritated her from the first day they met, but Dad pulled her aside and told her to be nice to him because he had a rougher path than most people. She tossed and turned so much Teller smacked her cheek with a paw before he stalked out of her room.

When Mom and Uncle Jimmy confronted Tina, she had, of course, denied she was responsible for the specter. Mom tried to point out she didn't think Tina was doing it consciously, but Tina ended the conversation and told them to leave when Mila woke up at the heated discussion.

Kirsten's alarm went off, dragging her from what little fitful sleep she could manage. She blearily shuffled to the bathroom to start her day.

When she headed downstairs fifteen minutes later, Teller was curled up on the corner of the couch. He opened one eye, yawned, and went back to sleep. Apparently, she wasn't forgiven for her restless night yet.

"You're going to have to pick up breakfast on the way to school," Mom said briskly as she slung on her coat. "My carton of eggs disappeared last night. I already loaded this week's allowance on yours and Kaley's debit cards. Make sure you place your order on the app so Jo can have your order ready."

"Where are you going?" Kirsten asked.

"Pomerene." Mom made a face. "I'm watching Amelia until you get out of school."

"Mom, I have conditioning after school," Kirsten protested. "And how am I getting to the hospital if you have your car?"

"I meant when you're done with conditioning." Mom shook her head. "You'll have the car. Tell Kaley to grab a ride home with Donny and pay for his gas. Is pizza from McKelvey's enough of a bribe for you three?"

"It means extra laps, but it's a deal." Kirsten grinned. "Who's watching Noah and Mila?"

A hint of sadness floated across Mom's face. "Tina's staying home with Noah today. Poor kid was running a fever yesterday at school, which was why she left work early."

"She'll forgive you," Kirsten murmured. "Eventually."

Mom snorted. "You didn't see her last night."

"You've looked out for her for the last twenty years." Kirsten shook her head. "She's an adult. You can't blame yourself when she disregards your advice. Or are you going to hold it against me and Kaley if we don't agree with you?"

Mom gave her a long measured look before she said, "You know, I hate it when you use my own words against me."

"I know." Kirsten crossed the kitchen and hugged Mom. "But they were good words."

Mom chuckled while she returned the embrace. "Brat. I'm glad you get along with the rest of the basketball team."

Kirsten snorted as they release each other. "Coach Park doesn't play favorites or put up with any mean girl crap."

"See you later this afternoon." Mom grabbed her laptop case.

"Wait, who's relieving me tonight?"

Mom turned back. "Thad's in town visiting Julia. He volunteered."

Kirsten whistled softly. "Is that a good idea if the Ryders have an eclectic?"

Mom shrugged. "He may work for the West Coast vampires, but the East Coast vamps aren't stupid enough to start something when the West Coast is run by gods. If this Kowalski bitch is stupid enough to harm Thad, there will be hell to pay in more ways than one. Now, I need to get going."

A few seconds after Mom charged out the back door, Kaley wandered into the kitchen with her backpack and still yawning.

"Why is there a sheriff's SUV parked in front of the house?"

"Mom's guarding Amelia today." Kirsten relayed the rest of Mom's instructions while she grabbed another carton of salt from Mom's supply cupboard.

"I hope she remembers to order an extra pizza for Donny." Kaley set her backpack on a chair, grabbed her varsity jacket, and held up the damaged sleeves. "I have no hope of earning enough money to replace my jacket if Tina refuses to use me for babysitting anymore."

"There's other places to get a job in town," Kirsten said sourly as she placed the salt in her backpack and zipped it.

"I've got to be careful where I apply," Kaley shot back. "Remember what happened during that field trip to the Victorian House Museum."

"Mom and Jo told us since we were little not to acknowledge any of the ghosts in town." Kirsten slung on her own coat and grabbed her backpack and gym bag. "Can we please go? I'm starving."

Kaley donned her own jacket and grabbed her backpack and gym bag. "Can I drive?"

"No, it's my turn."

"What if I need to leave school early?"

"Don't worry." Kirsten smirked. "The entire girls basketball team will be in the girls locker room so you don't get beat up by Jennifer and Madison."

"What if the Ryders' eclectic is behind the whole mess?" Kaley followed Kirsten out the back door. "Why else would someone pull Donny into this? Amelia and her crew tried to bully him, too. Plus, Tina didn't remember him though she's met him a couple of times at our house."

Kirsten considered the question as she locked the back door. "What if Tina lied about not remembering Donny? What if she lied to Uncle Jimmy and Mom last night about not being responsible for the specter?"

"But why?" Kaley marched to the rear of Mom's sedan. "What the hell is her motive? The eclectic has one. She's getting paid by Amelia's dad, and he'll do anything Amelia wants."

Kirsten popped the trunk lid, they both threw their bags and packs in, and Kirsten slammed the lid shut. "What are we missing? It's like there's something in front of us, and we can't see it."

"Let's get coffee and something to eat," Kaley said. "Maybe that will jumpstart your genius brain cells."

"You're just as smart as I am." Kirsten stomped to the driver side door and yanked it open.

"Yeah, but I like having a social life." Kaley slid into the passenger seat.

"You can do both," Kirsten snapped as she dropped into the driver seat and slammed the door.

"So can you," Kaley shot back. "But unlike you, I cannot be late to homeroom again."

"Then stop gossiping in the study hall until the second bell rings." Kirsten hit the ignition button. She was definitely going to need extra caffeine to get through this day.

Chapter 20

Kaley stomped into homeroom. Mrs. Thomas frowned, and her gaze dropped to Kaley's coffee cup. The teacher cleared her throat.

Even though Mrs. Thomas was Mom's age, she acted so much older. She wore neatly pressed pantsuits. She pulled her hair into a facelift tight bun. And she carried a military-level need for discipline, though in her case, it was semi-understandable. She retired from the army after putting in a full twenty years.

It took everything Kaley had not to roll her eyes. Mrs. Thomas may be strict, and she loved to dish out detention for what she called attitude from any student. But Kaley gave the teacher credit. She didn't play favorites like other people on the high school staff.

"I'm sorry." Kaley dropped her backpack on her chair. "I'll finish it in the hallway."

"Thank you." Mrs. Thomas nodded.

Kaley stepped out of the classroom with her cinnamon latte. Some students rushed up and down the hallway. Some stood by their lockers and gossiped. They all looked like they were ready for the weekend, even though it had been a four-day week.

Donny walked up to her while she gulped her coffee. "Got your text. So we're back to square one, huh?"

She shrugged. "Yeah. Mom's playing bodyguard this morning. Kaley's going to relieve her."

Donny scowled. "While I'm not one to turn down McKelvey's, are you sure leaving Kirsten at the hospital by herself is a good idea?"

"Believe it or not, it was Mom's idea." Kaley took another swig of her latte. "Because Kirsten is so much better—"

Donny kicked her heel hard enough to break her sibling rivalry rant. She looked in the direction he was staring.

Jennifer Rudlow and Madison Kenney walked toward them, nasty expressions on both girls' faces.

"What was your sister doing in Amelia's room at the hospital yesterday?" Jennifer spat. Everyone in the hallway watched, anticipating the fight turning physical.

"Guarding her ass," Kaley snapped.

"Or was she really there to hurt Amelia?" Madison sneered.

"You are both idiots." Kaley turned away from them.

Jennifer reached out and smacked Kaley's hand holding her coffee. Her cup flew into the air.

Before the coffee spilled, Kaley reached out with her abilities and solidified the air around the cup. There was a sharp inhalation from all the nearby students.

Mrs. Thomas stepped out of her classroom, reached up, and clasped the coffee cup. "Ms. Wilson, I'll give you a pass this one time. Go into the classroom and finish your drink." She handed it to Kaley. "Ms. Rudlow, Ms. Kenney, I believe you belong in another homeroom. I suggest you get going before you're late."

As if on cue, the first bell rang. The two cheerleaders scurried off. The rest of their audience broke up and headed toward their own homerooms.

"I'll catch you after practice tonight, Kaley." Donny nodded and strode down the hall.

"Thank you, Mrs. Thomas," Kaley said.

The teacher smiled at her. "I didn't like bullies when I was your age." She glanced in the direction Jennifer and Madison had taken. "It appears my opinion hasn't changed." She turned back to Kaley. "Like I said, this is a one-time pass on drinks in my classroom."

"Yes, ma'am." Kaley bobbed her head. "Thank you."

But she had a feeling her teacher had only delayed the inevitable confrontation with Amelia Ryder's crew.

Kaley spent the rest of the day, waiting to be jumped. Hope Stillwell had witnessed the incident with the other cheerleaders since she was in Mrs. Thomas's homeroom, too. The girls' varsity basketball team acted as Kaley's escort the rest of the morning. She couldn't even get mad at her twin about it because Kirsten didn't know what happened until Kaley texted her between third and fourth periods.

Amelia's boyfriend Brad and his cronies made a few loud, nasty cracks at lunch as they passed by Kaley's table and purposely sat near them. Donny got up and stalked over to the other football players' table on the pretense of discussing this afternoon's practice. Since it was a full-pad practice, he asked if everyone was up-to-date on their rabies vaccines because if anyone else came after Kaley again, they would get bit.

The tables around Brad and the other football players laughed their butts off, including Kirsten and her basketball buddies. Kaley prayed Donny hadn't just made things worse.

You need to chill and show you aren't afraid of them, Kirsten lectured silently.

For the brain in the family, you aren't that bright, Kaley snapped back. *Amelia, Jennifer, and Madison having been trying to goad me into using my craft against them since they found out I'm a witch.*

During her study hall, Kaley texted Mom about the incident. However, her only advice was to steer clear of the troublemakers. When Kaley asked if she'd be allowed to continue babysitting for Tina's kids, Mom texted that she hadn't talked to Tina yet, but she would call her this afternoon.

Between Mrs. Thomas's warning, Donny's threat and the varsity protection detail, no one bugged Kaley the rest of the day. Not even in the locker room after school.

Jennifer and Madison glared daggers at Kaley, but they didn't dare make a move with the girls' varsity basketball team present. And Kirsten hadn't been joking this morning about covering her butt in the locker room. The older girls got the junior varsity and freshmen girls to join them for cardio today.

When Kaley stepped out of the school and walked to the practice field, small white puffs chased, merged, and parted over the school. It was a little warmer today after the cold snap had followed Monday's storms. A downright pleasant day despite how the morning started.

It didn't make much of a difference during practice. Ms. Cross altered the routine so Mandy topped the cheerleaders' pyramid while ignoring Kaley unless she absolutely had to speak with her. At least, Jennifer and Madison were keeping their distance from Kaley, even after the basketball players finished their laps.

During their first water break, Kaley watched the football team's practice. Even though Donny wasn't allowed to play defense officially, the coach used him for drills. Donny had the strength to force the offense to play better, and unlike a lot of weres, he had the sense not to hurt someone. However, Donny went out of his way to scare Brad today. The quarterback scrambled like a rabbit getting chased by a, well, a coyote.

As she tucked her water bottle back in her bag, pale blue flashed in the corner of her eye. The specter ran silently onto the practice field and headed straight for Jennifer Rudlow.

Chapter 21

Kirsten pressed the icon for Mom's phone and waited for her to answer as she strode over to Mom's sedan.

"Hi, sweetie!"

"I'm on the way to the hospital," Kirsten said. "Be there in a few minutes."

"Did Kaley have any more problems at school?" Mom asked.

"Nope." Kirsten popped the trunk and tossed her bags in. "Hope is in Kaley's home room, so she and the rest of the team watched Kaley's back when Donny and I weren't around. Have you talked with Tina?"

"Yes, we spoke." Mom sighed. "She had her own issues with bullies in high school—"

Panicked screams and shouts came from the direction of the practice field.

"Kirsten?" Concern filled Mom's voice. "What's going on?"

"I may be a little late to the hospital." Kirsten ended the call and shoved her phone in her jeans pocket. Thank Goddess, she had replaced the canister of salt in her backpack this morning. She unzipped it and snatched the blue and white cardboard package out of her bag before she slammed the trunk lid shut and ran for the field. Adrenaline lent her tired muscles new energy.

She rounded the corner in time to see Kaley throw up a ward around the huddled cheerleaders and coach. And like at the hospital last night, the fake specter wore a four-legged form. Her gut clenched. The thing's body was distinct enough under the fading autumn light to resemble Donny's coyote side. It snapped and pawed at Kaley's ward. Blue and yellow sparks flew every time the fake specter touched the half-sphere.

While the rest of the football team gaped in shock, Donny raced toward the girls, ripping his equipment and clothes off as he ran. Fur sprouted from his skin. Muscle and bones shifted. His face elongated into a muzzle. He stopped his transformation at the half-way point, which was difficult as heck from what Kirsten had read. Thank Goddess, he left his practice pants on. Donny howled at the fake specter.

Kirsten skidded to a halt beside one of the coolers holding drinks for the football players. She poured salt on the lid and concentrated. While the field itself had excellent drainage, puddles from Monday's rain were still scattered around the edges. She pulled that water to her. The tendrils lapped up the salt off the cooler lid.

The fake specter backed away from the cheerleaders and faced Donny. It shrieked in response to the were's challenge.

Kirsten lashed out with a tendril of salt water. The fake specter shrieked again. Its features fizzed around the edge where she struck it.

Donny! Drive it in my direction! We need to keep it off balance! The last thing she needed was the fake specter to start throwing football equipment toward her or anyone else. The steel sleds holding the huge blocking dummies could crush someone.

Donny ran between Kirsten and the fake specter and snapped at it. The fake specter recoiled and dodged as if it feared being bitten. Now, why would it react that way?

Coach Cowher! The head football coach jerked at Kirsten's

voice in his mind. *Get the rest of the players off the field while Donny and I distract it!*

"We can't leave you two out here alone with that thing!" he yelled out loud and in her mind. "And the girls—"

They're going with you, Kirsten replied. *Kaley—*

I'm ready.

Kirsten lashed at the fake specter again when it turned toward the cowering cheerleaders behind her sister. It cried out again, but this time, it sounded more like a child's wail of pain.

The coaches and football players cleared the practice field and raced for the high school, but Coach Cowher stopped at the corner closest to the cheerleader's benches with a worried look on his face. The glowing blue canine noticed and stalked toward the coach.

Donny darted between the apparition and Cowher. The were howled a challenge. The fake specter snapped at him and connected. Donny tumbled to the ground with a whimper.

Kaley dropped her ward. Ms. Cross and the rest of the cheerleaders tore across the green and brown grass after the football team. Unfortunately, their movement caught the fake specter's attention. It pivoted and took a couple of running steps toward the defenseless Normals. The blocking pads abandoned along the sidelines started to quiver.

Kirsten gestured and a tendril of salt water wrapped itself around the fake specter's neck. It screamed, the sound more human than before. The water tendril froze and snapped. The fake specter whirled for Kaley—

And vanished.

Kirsten panted, trying to calm the adrenaline overloading her body while keeping control of her salt water tendrils. Still furry, Donny climbed slowly to his feet and cradled his left arm.

"What did you do?" Kaley called as she jogged toward them. In the distance, sirens wailed from the direction of town. "How did you get it to leave?"

"I thought you did it." Confusion raced through Kirsten. "What the heck just happened?"

Donny's face returned to its human appearance, and his fur faded. "Did either of you notice how it looked like me and sounded like a little kid?"

Kirsten and Kaley stared at each other.

"No." Kaley shook her head. "That doesn't make any sense."

"It's got to be Mila or Noah," Kirsten said. "Who else could it be?"

"But Tina's not that powerful a witch despite Mom and Jimmy's suspicions," Kaley protested. "How could either kid have that kind of power?"

"Come on, Kaley." Donny frowned at her. "Are we really going to judge a supernatural by his parents?"

Kaley blushed. "I'm sorry."

Two Holmes County Sheriff's Department vehicles squealed to a stop at the edge of the drive leading to the practice field. Uncle Jimmy baled out of his SUV, ignored all the coaches by the high school doors, and ran toward the girls and Donny.

"Are you three all right?"

Donny held up his injured arm. "Frostbite, but it'll heal up in an hour or two."

"Everyone else is fine," Kirsten said. "The more important thing is we know who's behind the specter now."

Chapter 22

Kaley drove while Kirsten made the requisite phone calls. Jo would pick up Mom from the hospital and meet them out at Tina's trailer. Donny sat in the back of the car, munching on a bag of fast food cheeseburgers. His were metabolism had kicked into high gear to deal with his injury, and he pointed out Kaley owed him for covering her ass on the practice field.

Basically, her babysitting wages from Monday now sat in Donny's stomach.

Kirsten's phone beeped as she ended the last call. "The high priestess has signed off on Mom's solution."

"I still don't like the idea of binding the kids' powers," Kaley grumbled. In fact, the proposal sat like a lead weight in her gut.

"You think terrorizing the Normals is a better solution?"

Kaley could feel her sister's gaze bore into her. She sighed. "No, that's not what I'm saying. They need to be taught to control their abilities, just like Mom did with us."

"Tina would need to give up finding another man and spend time with her kids." Kirsten snorted. "Think she's really going to do that?"

Kaley gritted her teeth. Kirsten made her feelings regarding Tina's dating habits clear, but Kaley didn't like her sister's judgy attitude.

"No one taught Tina until she was out of high school," Kaley said. "Maybe it's her lack of a good role model that's the problem."

"Mom taught Tina everything she knows," Kirsten snapped. "Are you saying Mom's not a good role model?"

"No, that's not what I'm saying," Kaley bit back.

Donny leaned between the two bucket front seats. "Speaking as someone without a good role model, Tina may not know what to teach her kids anymore than my mother. Mom does the best she can for not being a were. It took me a few years to understand that. Tina was raised by Normals in the foster system. Both my mom and Tina can love the hell out of their kids, but they are going to screw up once in a while because they don't know the right questions, much less the right people, to ask." He leaned back again and unwrapped another cheeseburger.

Kaley blinked and tightened her grip on the steering wheel. That was the longest she'd ever heard him speak at one time. And he was totally right.

Jo's little bright blue Honda was already sitting in the Eisler's driveway when Kaley pulled in behind it. The three of them climbed out of Mom's sedan and trooped up the short steps to the tiny porch.

Tina opened the front door. Her eyes were red and puffy. "I'm so sorry my kids tried to hurt you." Fresh tears trickled down her pale cheeks as she stepped back to let them in. Mom sat on the couch while Jo leaned back in the matching armchair.

"We don't think it was both of them," Kaley said gently. "Was Noah asleep around three-thirty this afternoon?"

Tina closed the front door. "Y-y-yes."

"Then he's probably our dreamwalker." Kaley wrapped her arm around Tina's shoulders. "If he's got the flu, too, it makes it harder to control abilities like dreamwalking."

"Is everyone at the high school okay?" Mom asked.

"I'm the only one who got hurt," Donny said.

"Oh, Goddess!" Tina put her hands over her mouth.

"Don't worry, Ms. Eisler. I'm already healed." Donny flexed his right arm, showing off his bicep beneath his t-shirt.

Tina lowered her hands. "That explains his nightmare. He hasn't stop talking about you since you came over the other night. How cool it would be to be a were. He woke up screaming that he was trying to protect Kaley from the mean cheerleaders, but he accidentally hurt you."

"Did he know about my run-in with Jennifer and Madison this morning?" Kaley asked.

Mom and Tina exchanged guilty looks.

"He, uh, overheard me talking to your mom on the phone," Tina admitted.

"Uh, Tina?" Kirsten stared out the front windows. "Is Noah asleep now?"

"I think so." Her voice trailed off.

Kaley turned to see what had distracted them. A glowing pale blue canine prowled among the cars in the driveway.

Jo pulled a couple of sage sticks out of her pocket. "Rachel."

Mom caught the one Jo tossed to her.

Mila chose that moment to run screaming from her room. "Mom! Mom! The ghost is out there again!"

Kirsten scooped the little girl into her arms. "Shhh." She laid her index finger across the child's lips. "It's okay. We know what's happening. We just need to fix it."

"I don't get it," Kaley said. "Why is he scaring his little sister?"

"He isn't doing it deliberately," Jo said as she lit the end of her white sage. "Mila simply saw his dream form coming and going."

"Kaley, get Tina's vacuum and start sweeping up the cumin

and salt you laid down over here." Mom gestured at an empty spot of the wall inset with the windows.

"But if I do, Noah's dream self could hurt all of you," Kaley protested.

"No, sweetie." Jo smiled as she handed her lighter to Mom. "It's been trying to get back to Noah the last couple of days. That's the reason he's sick."

"But what about Miz Rose and the mess he made at her place?" Kirsten asked.

"We'll ask him when he wakes up." Mom blew out the flame on her stick. Sage smoke curled to the ceiling. "For now, please do as I ask."

Kaley raced down the short hall to the utility closet, pulled out Tina's little upright, and unwound the cord as she dragged it into the living room. She tossed the plug to Donny, who knelt and inserted it into the outlet. She pushed the power switch, praying Noah's dream self didn't interfere with the electric supply to the house.

The blue dream coyote perked its ears when the vacuum roared to life. It stalked toward the trailer.

Kaley quickly vacuumed that section of the carpet. The dream coyote leapt right through the wall and landed in front of her. Mila emitted a muffled cry. Mom yanked Kaley back and inserted herself between Kaley and the dream coyote.

It seemed to glare at Mom. She gestured with her left hand and created a smoke shield similar to the one Kaley had used at Miz Rose's. But this one curved, only giving the dream coyote access to the bedrooms and bath.

"Time to rejoin your boy, my little friend," Mom crooned.

The dream coyote shook itself before it trotted through the

interior wall separating the living room from Noah's room. A moment late, a hoarse voice called out, "Mom."

Mom smiled at Tina. "I think that's your cue."

Over take-out McKelvey's pizza supplied by Uncle Jimmy, the female Wilsons relayed the afternoon's events to him and Dad.

"So this dream wolf—" Dad started.

"Dream coyote," Kaley corrected.

"Dream coyote won't show up again?" Dad finished.

"Not accidentally anyway." Mom poured more diet cola into her glass. The liquid fizzed and popped as it released its carbon dioxide. "Noah's going to need a lot of extra training. One of the elders is coming down to evaluate his skills and aptitude this weekend."

"What do we do in the meantime?" Uncle Jimmy asked around a huge mouthful of pizza.

Mom groaned. "This isn't a see-food dinner, Jimmy. And we don't need to do a darn thing." She took a sip of her diet cola. "His powers are bound until he can get a handle on them."

"I don't get how he's so much more powerful than Tina," Dad said.

"Genetics." Mom shrugged. "There's a lot of folks who may be carrying supernatural genes and don't know it. My guess is Ken Eisler might be one of them."

"Why was the kid's dream coyote going after certain people?" Dad asked.

"A lot of it was repressed anger over his parents' divorce,"

Kaley said. "That gave his dream self certain characteristics of a poltergeist."

"Which was part of the reason the dream self was hanging out at Miz Rose's," Kirsten added. "He joined 4-H when she was our advisor. She retired about the same time Tina and Ken filed for divorce. Part of Noah didn't think it was fair he'd lost most of the important people in his life at the same time."

"And he resented Miz Rose leaving to spend more time with her grandchildren since she was the closest thing he had to a grandmother," Kaley said.

"He told you all of this." Uncle Jimmy looked at her askance.

"No, Donny talked to him." Kaley reached for another slice from the pizza box in the middle of the table. "Guy to guy. Noah's hero worship of Donny is why the dream form changed from a child-sized blob to a coyote."

"What about the Ryder girl?" Dad prompted.

Jimmy snorted. "No magick there. Just her own stupidity. I did have a little talk with Art Ryder's eclectic. Kowalski admitted Amelia had approached her about hexing Kaley, but she didn't give Amelia anything. After Art approached her about protecting Amelia from Kaley, Kowalski told him about Amelia's request for a hex. Apparently, Kowalski has limits."

He grabbed another slice. "What I don't get is why Noah's dream form went after Jennifer Rudlow?"

"He overheard Tina and me talking about Kaley getting harassed by Jennifer and Madison today," Mom said. "Since Amelia couldn't do anything while she was in the hospital, his dream self turned its attention to the more immediate threat."

"Also, Noah was in the room when I told Kirsten about my suspension." Kaley sprinkled grated parmesan on her pizza before she held the cheese canister out to Jimmy. He shook his head. "Unfortunately, he also has a bit of a crush on me, so part of him wanted to be my knight in shining armor."

"That's a lot of parts for one little boy," Dad commented.

"Everybody has a lot of parts to them." Mom smiled. "It's just that for supernaturals, the other parts sometimes come out to play. I'm just happy this whole thing is over."

Kaley glanced at Kirsten, who rolled her eyes. Nope, this wasn't over. Not by a long shot. Not when fifty of their classmates and teachers saw them and Donny use their powers right out there in public.

The only question was how bad would it get and whether they'd survive until graduation.

Chapter 23

Two weeks later, Kirsten waited nervously on the uncomfortable black and aluminum chair outside of Sheriff James H. Birkheimer's office in the department building. While the red brick exterior made the place look imposing, the stark white interior had almost an antiseptic quality.

Like a mental hospital.

It didn't help that the sheriff's administrative assistant kept shooting Kirsten suspicious glances.

Finally, the door opened and two deputies stepped out. Julia Wolford winked at her while the male deputy gave her a friendly nod.

"Come on in, Ms. Wilson!" Uncle Jimmy beckoned with the first two fingers of his right hand.

Kirsten rose and smoothed her pantsuit. Dad had said to dress up for this appointment, but skirts and dresses were so not her thing. And Dad weirdly added to call Uncle Jimmy by his title. When she entered the sheriff's office, she was surprised to find Millersburg Police Chief Patricia Hall already seated in one of the guest chairs.

"Have you met Chief Hall?" he asked.

"No, sir." Kirsten held out her hand. "A pleasure, ma'am."

The chief's grip was firm and without the need to prove something like a lot of guys' handshakes. "I've heard a lot of good thing about you, Ms. Wilson. Are the Lady Knights going to the state final four this year?"

"We're planning to go all the way, ma'am." Kirsten grinned.

"Have a seat, Ms. Wilson," Jimmy said. When she did so, he asked, "Have you decided on your college plans yet?"

"They aren't finalized." Kirsten looked at Chief Hall, then back at Jimmy. "What exactly is going on? My dad wasn't specific about what this meeting concerned."

Chief Hall spoke up. "Our respective departments have been discussing the supernatural situation. We may not have the problems the big cities do, but that doesn't mean we don't have our issues."

"You mean like Noah Eisler?" Kirsten said.

"That was a kid who needed the right help," Jimmy said. "We're talking about domestic abuse where one of the partners is a supernatural or—" He grimaced. "—the Killbuck pack running drugs."

"We're putting together a joint task force specifically for these types of problems," Chief Hall continued. "The problem is we don't have any supernaturals in either of our departments."

Kirsten's suspicions immediately flared. "And you want a token supernatural?"

Both law officers laughed. "Told you that's what she'd say," Jimmy said.

"Not a token." Chief Hall turned serious. "It's hard enough recruiting anyone from outside to live in a village our size." She gestured at the sheriff. "Jimmy suggested we recruit from younger members of the county while we also do an outside search."

"And the reason I asked about your college plans is we got the county commissioners as well as the mayor and city council to pony up the money for a paid internship." Jimmy leaned his elbows on his desk. "But they insist the person needs to be enrolled in criminal justice at a local college."

"Be straight with me, Sheriff Birkheimer." Kirsten cocked her head. "Did Dad put you up to this?"

Chief Hall cleared her throat. "Actually, I did. I saw the video of you in action, saving your classmates from that ghost dog. And I've seen you play sports your entire high school career. You keep your head when the chips are flying, and that's one of the biggest assets any law enforcement officer can have in their repertoire."

"Plus the internship won't start until after basketball season," Sheriff Birkheimer answered.

"But I just turned seventeen, and I'm not in college yet," Kirsten protested.

"Age won't be the issue as long as you start taking college classes, which according to your parents, your guidance counselor is pushing for next year anyway," Jimmy said. "Ashland is holding a slot in their criminal justice program for our intern. You can take a part-time schedule online. Your first year classes are the basic curriculum no matter what your major is. If in the end, you decide not to go to Ashland after you graduate, you can transfer the hours to most colleges."

"That's . . . a lot to think about," Kirsten said. "What happens in the meantime if you find a full-time adult?"

"The money's already been allocated for both in next year's budget," Chief Hall answered.

"This would be an incredible opportunity for anyone. Can I have some time to think it over?" Kirsten asked.

"Sure," Jimmy and Chief Hall chorused.

After another round of handshakes and making sure she had the law officers' numbers, Kirsten walked out to Mom's sedan on shaky legs. She'd considered criminal justice and maybe a law degree before applying for the FBI. However, she always saw herself dong it in another state. Someplace she could make her mark without always being compared to Kaley.

Somehow, it seemed the Universe was trying to show her that she was valued for herself and not as one of a set. Maybe this was an opportunity she needed to seize.

Kirsten pushed the ignition button of Mom's sedan. If she was doing an internship, she'd need her own car.

That was the first thing to mention to Mom and Dad tonight at dinner.

Check out Kirsten and Kaley's next adventure, *Fae and Felonies*! Can the girls handle their family's bigotry, and their own, when a new kid who's fae moves into town? Turn the page for a sneak peek!

Fae and Felonies

Kaley Wilson scribbled frantically on her trig worksheet. The white paper practically glowed underneath the energy efficient LED fixtures. The damn light didn't feel natural. The softer yellow ones would have been much more comfortable to both Normal and witch eyes, but West Holmes School District had to go with the lowest bidder.

What was the formula for a tangent again? She ignored classmates filtering into homeroom as she flipped through her notes, but she couldn't filter out their scents. Nothing like the scent of manure on boots to overpower the stink of dry-erase markers and ruin one's concentration.

She found the right page, scribbled down the correct formula, and started working through the next equation. How could she be an identical twin, yet advanced math was a breeze for Kirsten? And her sister refused to help her with homework last night.

Okay, maybe she shouldn't have been catching up on the post boys' basketball game gossip with Bella Sims until midnight before she asked Kirsten for assistance. Kaley realized she forgot to carry the one and scrubbed the mistake with her eraser. If only Principal Reed hadn't suspended her from cheerleading for the week for skipping study hall on Monday. But no, Reed still held a grudge over his attempt to suspend her for fighting when all she did was step out of the way of a blow fellow cheerleader Amelia Ryder aimed at her head in the girl's locker room, so he refused to overlook one little misstep.

If Mom and Dad wouldn't have grounded her, she could have snuck into the game, picked up some details about Brad and Amelia's breakup, flirted with Josh Fairbanks a bit, and gotten her homework done, instead of fretting in her bedroom the entire night about the whole situation. Kaley was pretty certain Josh was into her, but for all his exploits on the football field, he was shy when it came to the opposite gender. He just needed a little encouragement.

Crap! She used the formula for sine, not cosine. She flipped her pencil and erased the two lines she'd screwed up.

And who the heck needed trigonometry anyway? No one used it in fashion marketing.

As she tried to explain to Mom and Dad, who refused to listen.

Hope Stillwell nudged Kaley's arm with the eraser end of her pencil.

"Stop it!" Kaley hissed without looking up. "I'm trying to get this last problem—"

"Hottie at two o'clock."

Kaley looked up at the same moment alien magick tingled across her skin, raising the hairs on her arms and legs. A chill ran through her. She didn't need the feel of his power to know the boy staring at her was fae. The white shock of hair wasn't a color you saw on most Normals, even with the help of modern dyes.

The fae was tall as most Unseelie were. His platinum hair made his tanned skin stick out and accented his brilliant blue eyes. He actually wore jeans and a sweatshirt under his coat, instead of glamouring Normal clothing. He had been staring at her, but quickly dropped his gaze and stalked to the back of the room. So he knew what she was, too.

Worry gripped her, and she automatically solidified her mental and magickal shields. The last thing they needed was even an incidental interaction between their energies. The mix wasn't like oil and water. It was more like matter and anti-matter. And such an interaction usually resulted in the death of both the witch and the fae in question. In this close of quarters, they could take out their teacher and the entire class, too.

After the Battle of Millersburg, why the hell would the Winter Queen break the truce by sending one of her people to Holmes County?

Kaley resisted the urge to turn around and look at him again. The fae aged at a much slower rate than humans, even those with longer lifespans like witches and weres, so he could be older than her great-aunt Jo. The only people comparable to the fae where the vampires, and the fae viewed them as diseased cheaters because their extended life was courtesy of the V-virus.

"Why would someone change schools this late in the year?" Hope whispered.

"The middle of November isn't that late in the school year," Kaley whispered back. "And he may not have had a choice." Which was true if he was under orders from the Winter Queen.

Kaley turned back to the problem, but her concentration was totally destroyed. The bell rang, and Mrs. Thomas started calling roll. She'd have to take the hit on her homework score.

But that didn't bother her as much as the fae sitting behind her.

Kaley spotted her identical twin sister in the cafeteria. Well, identical if Kaley didn't dye her hair blond. Kirsten kept the rich mahogany color they'd been born with, the same shade as Mom and Aunt Jo's hair.

Kirsten sat with Hope and the rest of the varsity girl's basketball team. Kaley charged over to their table and plopped down across from her sister. "I need to tell you something—"

"I'm not doing your damn homework." Kirsten glared at her as she shoved a forkful of green beans into her mouth.

"No," Kaley snapped. "There's a new boy—"

"Crap!" Hope grinned. "I forgot to tell you about the hot guy who showed up in trig class this morning."

"Tall and cute in an emo way," Olivia Burke added in a dreamy voice. Her reaction didn't make sense. She didn't swing toward boys.

Kirsten looked at Olivia, frowned, and looked back at Kaley. *What's going on?* she asked telepathically.

He's fae.

"You're kidding, right?" Kirsten said aloud. Her brown eyes widened, and worry flowed past her mental shields. Kaley was fairly certain her sister's expression was the same one she had on her face before the morning bell.

"Not about this," she said. *I texted Jo between classes, but I haven't gotten an answer yet.*

"Why would anyone want to move here this late in the school year?" Kirsten said.

Hope made a face. "That's what I said."

Kirsten ignored her friend. "You think he's related to the guys who messed with the Amish years ago?"

Kaley shrugged. "Because of the murders, the corridor project stalled. They did invest a ton of money into the commercial properties that would have adjoined the exit ramps."

"What the heck are you guys talking about?" Olivia looked at Kaley and Kirsten like they spoke in a foreign language.

"Some ancient family history—" Kirsten's expression changed from contemplative to solemn. "The principal is walking this way. Behave yourself."

Kaley resisted the urge to roll her eyes. She looked over her shoulder as his shadow fell across her.

"Good afternoon, ladies." Principal Reed's voice was genial, but the emotion never reached his eyes. "Kirsten, we have a new student River Martin who started today. I need you to meet with him after school. Help him get caught up."

She cocked her head. "You do realize I have basketball practice?"

"It doesn't start until three-thirty, which is forty-five minutes after school ends." His tone didn't leave any room for Kirsten to argue.

She plastered on a fake smile. "All right. Tell him to meet me in the library. But it'll have to be thirty-five minutes so I have a chance to change and warm up."

"Fine," Principal Reed said.

Kaley watched him stroll toward Amelia Ryder who was sitting at a nearby table with the rest of the cheerleading squad. Well, technically, Amelia was sitting in her decorated wheel chair.

"He could have at least said 'please' and 'thank you,'" Kirsten grumbled under her breath while he attempted to flirt with the cheerleaders. His whole act made Kaley sick to her stomach. Good grief, the man was old enough to be the girls' grandfather.

Hope shook her head. "That would mean acknowledging us as real people."

"Still this is our chance to check out the new kid," Kaley said as she turned back to her sister.

Kirsten's jaw worked before she said, "Think you can get Donny to come with us when we meet this new guy?"

Kaley considered her words. Kirsten was totally oblivious to Donny Fryer's crush on her. Donny threatened to bite Kaley if she said anything. Yet, her sister kept asking for his help with supernatural matters though she claimed he was trouble like the remaining werecoyotes in Holmes County.

"I can ask him," Kaley said. "But why?"

Kirsten scowled. "If we can't defend ourselves, Donny can rip the new kid's throat out."

Acknowledgements

Many thanks to my friend Valerie Lennox, who designed these covers just as I toyed with the idea of writing about Rachel Wilson's twin daughters. And much gratitude to my formatter JW Manus for finding the most appropriate ornaments for the interiors of the Millersburg Magick Mysteries.

Hugs and kisses to my support team, Darling Husband, Princess Bella, Genius Kid, and the Grandpuppy. Thanks especially to my bipedal family. I didn't need those Reese's Pieces on my waist!

The COVID-19 pandemic struck as I originally wrote this book in particular. I finished the next two stories, but I'll tell you something.

Depression lies.

And I didn't realize that I was suffering from low-level depression, like a good chunk of the rest of the world. Not to mention, the shutdowns happened a month before my two-year cancer-versary while I was still undergoing treatment. It was just a bad time.

Once the snow melted, and the flowers bloomed in the backyard, my mental space started to readjust. I took a hard look at what I'd written since the start of shutdowns.

The first half of *Spells and Sleuths*, the chapters I'd written prior to the shutdowns looked pretty good. The rest?

Let's just say it didn't match the light-hearted, Scooby-Doolike tone I had been originally aiming for. So, I unpublished the Millersburg Magick Mysteries with the intent to re-write them. And every time I sat down to do so, I had one or more major life events.

Until now.

I also apologize to the folks who started to read this series, only to have me rip them away without warning. I didn't think anyone was actually looking at them. However, the last thing I wanted to do was turn into George Lucas. (Han shot first, dammit!) But I did it anyway.

And I really, truly won't ever do that to you again. Cross my heart.

About the Author

Suzan Harden transitioned from writing information technology manuals for companies and legal articles for a law enforcement magazine to her first love, fantasy and science fiction in all their forms. She's the author of the Bloodlines, the 888-555-HERO, and the Justice series.